# MINOR MAGE

## T. KINGFISHER

*For our leathery leperous armadillo friends.*

# CONTENTS

Oliver was a very minor mage. His familiar reminded him of this several times a day.

He only knew three spells, and one of them was to control his allergy to armadillo dander. His attempts to summon elementals resulted in nosebleeds, and there is nothing more embarrassing than having your elemental leave the circle to get you a tissue, pat you comfortingly, and then disappear in a puff of magic. The armadillo had about wet himself laughing.

He was a very minor mage.

Unfortunately, he was all they had.

❦

They stood on the edge of the town: the boy, the armadillo, and the crowd. No one was moving. If an artist had painted the scene, it would have been *Still Life with Armadillo*, or perhaps *Mob Scene, Interrupted*.

Oliver looked at the crowd. Up until about an hour ago, they had been his friends and neighbors. Now they were familiar strangers, trying to look somber and serious and mostly just looking scared and a little uncertain. This was a bad thing to see on the faces of so many adults.

"Well go on, get moving," said Harold, the miller. "Sooner you get started, sooner we'll get rain."

He made a little shooing gesture, as if Oliver was a chicken that had wandered into the yard.

Harold the miller was not a handsome man, and less so when he was red with embarrassed anger, so Oliver turned and looked at the road instead.

It was an expanse of baked dust the color of bone. It wound between plowed fields for a little way, accompanied by drainage ditches full of nettles, then disappeared in the distance, over a hill and into the back of beyond. Far off in the distance, the bulk of the Rainblade Mountains were a dark blue shadow against the sky.

Oliver knew the farms that the road ran past, at least as far as the hill. After that, there were fallow fields, and after those... nothing.

Well, presumably there was *something*, but nobody went that way. It wasn't forbidden, it wasn't dangerous, it was just rather pointless. There wasn't anything there worth visiting.

The crowd of townspeople shifted nervously. Someone muttered something toward the back and was immediately hushed.

There is something about a group of people that is less than the sum of its parts. Few individuals in the crowd would have dreamed of putting a kid—even a kid who was also a mage— onto the road and telling him to bring back rain. And yet when they were all together, somehow the conversation had gotten more and more heated and more and more stern and what had been a vague idea became an order, and suddenly something slightly less than a mob but rather more than a friendly gathering of neighbors had arrived at the doorstep of Oliver's house. He'd been afraid the miller was going to drag him out of the house by the collar.

This was not something he'd ever worried about before, and he didn't much like it.

The most obnoxious thing about it all was that he'd been planning on going *anyway*.

You didn't need to be a wizard to know the crops did need rain. Even the fields near the road, watered painstakingly by hand, had a parched look. The leaves drooped limply, as if the plants were panting in the heat.

You didn't need to be a wizard to realize that if the rains didn't come, it was going to get very bad in the village.

But you also *definitely* didn't need to be a wizard to know that Oliver's mom was not going to let her twelve-year-old son hare off to the distant Rainblade Mountains, past bandits and monsters and lord knew what else.

His mother was a retired mercenary, but not so retired that she wouldn't have kicked and abused Harold twice around the village square for even suggesting such a thing. But she had gone up to Wishinghall to help his sister with the new baby, and she'd left him, because the village needed their mage, even a very minor one.

Oliver had started packing his bag almost as soon as she was out the door. He just hadn't expected to have the entire village turn up on the doorstep before he had a chance to leave.

The funny thing—not amusing, exactly, but funny none-theless—was that he'd been entirely willing to risk his life for the village, and now here they were, demanding that he do some-thing he'd been planning to do anyway, and apparently willing to throw him out on his ear if he didn't.

He'd be lying if he said that this hadn't soured his enthusiasm a bit.

"Err," said Vezzo. He had a farmer's tanned skin and broad, scarred hands. "Look, Oliver, it's not that we're happy about this, but you're the town wizard, and it's your job to bring the rains. Your predecessor made the journey to the Rainblades when he was young."

"How young?" asked Oliver, who had a pretty good idea of the answer.

"Err," said Vezzo, and appeared to find something fascinating stuck under his fingernails.

"Twenty-five," said the armadillo, who had been quiet up until now. "My mother was his familiar at the time."

"None of that," said Harold loudly, determinedly not looking at the armadillo. He'd never seemed to like Oliver's familiar, which was a major reason that Oliver didn't like *him*. "None of that now, boy. You're a wizard, you'll be just fine. And we're not forcing you. You're the wizard. It's your *job* to go."

And I was going! thought Oliver. I was trying to decide whether to pack three pairs of socks or only two, and then I was going to feed the chickens and head over to Vezzo's farm so that he could tell Mom where I'd gone!

Vezzo stood beside Harold. The farmer looked like an extremely uncomfortable ox, but like an ox, he was blocking Oliver's path.

"It *is* your job, Oliver," he said quietly. "I'm not happy about it, but we've got to have rain."

There were lines between the farmer's eyes, and deeper ones running in furrows from the sides of his nose, as deep as if he'd plowed them.

"You could have asked, you know," said Oliver a bit sadly. He had always liked Vezzo.

"It was supposed to just be asking," said the farmer. He leveled a bitter look at Harold. "Somehow it turned into more than that."

Oliver sighed. "It's fine," he said. "Just—*you* tell Mom, okay? Not him." He flapped a hand at Harold. "He'll come up with some stupid story about it to try to save his skin. You tell her how it really happened."

"Now see here—" Harold began, eyes nearly popping with outrage.

"I will," said Vezzo, ignoring the miller. "I promise, I'll tell

4

her exactly what happened. She'll be awfully mad, but I'll tell her anyway. You have my word."

He held out a hand.

Oliver shook. Vezzo's hand was almost twice the size of his and heavily callused.

The crowd, collectively, seemed to sigh. The armadillo also sighed and leaned his small armored body against Oliver's shins.

"Right, then," said Harold the miller. "If that's all settled—"

"Just stop," said Oliver. "Just... stop talking, okay? I'm going, all right? I was going to go anyway."

The miller might have had something to say about that, but Vezzo put a big hand on the man's shoulder and he fell silent. That was something of a relief.

Oliver looked over the crowd. None of them said anything. He saw his mother's friend, Matty, who was always baking, and who had brought him a meat pie yesterday for dinner, and even she wouldn't look at him. She was twisting her apron in her hands, and she looked like she was about to cry.

He spoke to her directly. "Matty—"

She looked up, biting her lip, and he realized at once that she was already crying.

"Will you make sure our chickens are fed while I'm gone?" he asked. Whatever he'd been about to say wasn't as important as the tears running down her face. "And water the garden, and—"

He ran out of things to say. The enormity of the fact that he was actually leaving choked him.

He'd been planning this for over two weeks, ever since his mom had said that she was going, and it still hadn't seemed real until right now. He almost wanted to cry himself, but not with everyone watching.

Matty nodded, made a small, miserable noise, and pulled her apron up to cover her face.

"Right, then," said Oliver. He hefted his pack. It was heavy, mostly from his dog-eared copies of the *Encyclopedia of Common Magic* and *101 Esoteric Home Recipes* and his mother's smallest copper cooking pot. He had a little money, and a little food, and three spells.

He hoped it would be enough.

"Be careful, Oliver," said Vezzo. "There's bad ground between here and there."

Oliver wanted to say, *Then why aren't you coming with me?* But he didn't, because he knew why. He was the wizard. He was what they had.

But he didn't quite trust himself to speak, so he turned away and started down the road. The armadillo trotted at his heels, like a small armored dog.

He looked back a few times, hoping that someone would dart out and say, "I'll come with you!" or "This is a mistake, come back!" but they didn't, and they vanished quickly, as if ashamed. Only Vezzo stayed in place, watching him go. He waved whenever Oliver looked back, and the third time, Oliver relented and lifted a hand in return, so that it would feel a little less like going into exile.

## ❧ 2 ❧

Oliver got half an hour down the road, brooding.

What had come over everyone? One day they'd been his neighbors, the people he grew up with, and then this morning they'd been...

He groped for a word inside his head. *Strange. Irrational. Scary.*

When Harold and Vezzo had shown up at the door and demanded that he go to the Rainblades, he'd tried to explain that he was going anyway, and it was like they hadn't even *heard* him.

It was the drought of course, but there had been droughts before, and people didn't get scary like this.

It must have been the clouds.

A week ago, the drought should have broken. The sky had filled up with thick clouds with dark blue-grey bottoms, and everyone had waited, because that meant rain. The village was almost silent with anticipation. You could have heard a raindrop fall anywhere in a five-mile radius, as people held their breath.

Except it hadn't.

The clouds had hung over the fields for most of a day, and then they had moved on, blown eastward by winds that herded and chided and chivvied them along. The edges of the clouds shredded into grey rags, and the sky behind them was hard and mercilessly blue.

The villagers could have handled lack of rain. Oliver was pretty sure that it was the *hope* of rain, snatched away, that had driven them over the edge.

He wondered if it had been like this when his predecessor had gone off to bring the rain back. Everybody talked about it like it had been a heroic act, but what if the old man had been sent off by farmers acting strangely too?

This was an unsettling thought.

And they never say how he did it, either. Just 'brought back the rain' and some talk about the Cloud Herders. What if it's a spell? What will I do if I get to the Rainblades and I'm not good enough to do it and the Cloud Herders won't give me the time of day?

He was worrying at this idea in his head when the armadillo tripped him.

Oliver yelped, arms windmilling, and only just managed to catch himself by hopping sideways on one foot.

"What was *that* for?" he asked irritably, glaring at his familiar.

The armadillo made an expansive gesture with a clawed paw. Oliver looked around.

There was nothing there. The fields stretched out in all directions, parched and tan. The town was visible as a large, mud-colored blotch behind him. The sky was a hard, brittle blue. It looked as if you could break your knuckles on it.

"What?"

"It's hot," said the armadillo. "Drink something."

"Oh." Now that Oliver thought about it, he was pretty thirsty. His head ached from more than brooding, and there was sweat soaking the collar of his shirt. He reached for the leather bottle hanging from his belt. "I hadn't thought of it."

"It's not good stomping along mad and forgetting to take care of yourself," said the armadillo.

"I'm not mad," said Oliver. "I mean, I was going to go *anyway*, but... well. Okay, I'm a little mad. Mostly at Harold." He sat down and took a drink of water, then stared at the open mouth of the bottle without really seeing it. "I just... what happened? They were acting like they were bewitched or something."

"They weren't," said the armadillo. "I mean, if you want my professional opinion."

"I know," said Oliver. "I didn't sneeze at all. If somebody'd bespelled them, my nose would be running like a sieve. It's just... I don't know." He rubbed his knuckles over his forehead.

He sat there for a few minutes, in the red darkness behind his eyes. After a bit, a long, scaly head thrust nonchalantly under his hand. Oliver scratched behind his familiar's ears. He was still a little angry, but he had to stick the anger somewhere in the back of his head so he didn't snap at people like the armadillo, who didn't deserve it.

Of course, that assumed there would be more people between here and the Rainblades.

A thought occurred to him. "Um. Armadillo?"

"Yes?"

"How do we get to the Rainblades? I mean, I see them now, but if there's someone we're supposed to talk to, or a road we're supposed to take..."

"Didn't your predecessor tell you?"

"Well, I'm sure he meant to." Oliver felt bad implying that the village's previous mage, that sweet old man, had shirked his duties. "But—err—well, his mind wandered a bit toward the end, and—"

"He was madder than a drunken mayfly," said the armadillo grimly. "He forgot that, too, huh?"

"I'm sure he meant to tell me." Oliver was determined to stand up for the old mage. He'd been extremely kind to a snot-nosed little kid who had magic coming off him in poltergeist fits, and Oliver had never forgotten that kindness, even when the old man had gone a bit barmy and had taken to wearing his underwear on his head.

"Three spells." The armadillo scuffled at the ground. "Three spells, and whatever you picked up from his ramblings. A child trained by a senile old man. It's a travesty. Still, I suppose you're what we've got."

Oliver reminded himself that he was not going to snap at the armadillo.

"Fortunately, in this case, my mother gave me a detailed description of the journey. I should be able to find the way." He paused, gazing at the distant shadow of the Rainblades. "I think."

That was not particularly comforting, but at least they weren't traveling completely blind. Oliver took a last drink from the water bottle and stood up, dusting himself off. The pale dust of the road clung to his trousers in cream-colored streaks.

"Did he tell you what to do when you got to the Rainblades?" asked the armadillo.

"Um." Oliver rubbed the back of his neck. It felt gritty. "Not exactly. It's where the Cloud Herders live though, isn't it?"

"Is it?"

"That's what everyone says."

"Well, far be it from me to argue with *everyone*."

Oliver knew the armadillo was being sarcastic, but he said, "I tried arguing with everyone. You saw how that went."

The armadillo muttered under his breath.

They kept walking.

*Well, on the bright side, at least if Mom thinks they forced me to leave, she'll be mad at Harold and not me.*

This was a very cheering thought. He was a bit frightened of the journey and (if he was being honest) more than a little frightened of what might lie at the journey's end, but both these things paled in comparison to fear of his mother's wrath.

*If she'd found out that he had snuck off to bring rain back...*

oh, hell. She *might* let him out of the house before he died of old age. If he was *lucky*.

But now he got to come back as the conquering hero. His mom would be glad to see him and wouldn't yell at him for leaving. Harold was going to take the heat, not him.

*Which he deserves. I'm pretty sure he tried to kick my familiar once when he thought I wasn't looking.*

Despite the heat, Oliver began to whistle.

*I wonder what the Cloud Herders will look like.*

The line of paw prints behind the armadillo began to weave back and forth across the road. Oliver reached down and scooped his familiar up in his arms.

"I can still walk," said the armadillo.

Oliver didn't say anything. Armadillos have their dignity. After a few moments, his familiar rested his armored cheek against Oliver's own and sighed.

⚜

"Master?" asked a very young Oliver, cradling the faintly damp warmth of a very young armadillo in his hands. "Can I ask a question?"

"You can always *ask,*" said the old wizard. "You *should* always ask, in fact. Questions make the world go round! Whether I've got an answer is another matter." He was having one of his good days, and his eyes were hard chips of sapphire in his wrinkled face.

The baby armadillo rolled over and snuffled at Oliver's fingers. Oliver exhaled in sheer wonder. He had known the young armadillo for less than two hours and loved him fiercely. Sure, he was a very, *very* young armadillo, and somewhat unfinished looking, but he was already cuter and more entertaining than the baby next door.

The baby next door would have been radically improved with claws and a snout, as far as Oliver was concerned.

"Why do we have familiars?"

"Do you not want one, then?" asked the old mage. "Bit late, I'd say."

"No!" Oliver clutched the armadillo to his chest, afraid that someone might snatch him away. The armadillo cheeped in protest, then dug with almost nonexistent claws at Oliver's shirt, seeking the protection of someplace dark and warm. "I want him! I'm not saying I don't! But why do we have familiars? What do they *do*?"

The old wizard grinned. The baby armadillo discovered the neck of Oliver's shirt and began burrowing determinedly down inside. Oliver felt him clamber down and settle into the hammock where Oliver's shirt was tucked into his pants.

He hoped that the armadillo wouldn't pee on him again. There were four armadillo kits in the litter, three of which were nursing quietly on their mother, the old wizard's familiar. The fourth had looked up when the door opened, let out a cheep, then wobbled determinedly across the floor to Oliver and peed on his foot.

"Well." The old man leaned down and petted his own elderly familiar, who was laying on her side, looking like a small, scaly footrest. "Familiars are important. They remember things we forget. Some of them—not armadillos, usually, but other kinds— act as your hands. Someday you'll be able move yourself into your familiar's mind and watch through their eyes." He stroked the mother armadillo's ears, and she snorted with pleasure.

"Mostly, though, they remind us that we're wizards..."

❧

The armadillo did not have a name, or rather, he had only one name, and that was enough.

His true name was Eglamarck. Oliver knew better than to bandy that name about in public, or indeed, any time when it wasn't strictly magically necessary. A familiar's true name was the key to what made it a familiar, instead of just another armadillo nosing around in the dry lands and licking up insects. It was not to be used lightly.

Since he had a name for the important things, the armadillo did not see the point of having another one merely for the convenience of his wizard. He was not a dog. He wasn't going to get saddled with a name like "Spot" or "Lucky" just so that he could be trotting back and forth at all hours when the name got called. If Oliver needed him, he'd be around.

Oliver's predecessor, who had Eglamarck's mother as a familiar for nearly seventy years, had told Oliver that it wasn't worth fighting over. For the few years that he had taught Oliver, his armadillo had been "my armadillo" and Oliver's had been "your young armadillo there." They'd managed.

Oliver had resigned himself to having a familiar who was effectively named "Armadillo."

His predecessor, that wonderful white-bearded old man, had told Oliver a lot of things. Unfortunately, he was nearly ninety by the time he'd taken on his last apprentice, and his mind wandered badly. He'd done his best, but some things he told Oliver four or five times, and many things he hadn't told him at all.

But he'd given the young mage all the books he had, and a small, scaly bundle of infant armadillo, and from those things, Oliver had learned enough that the townspeople had taken him as the new mage.

It hadn't been too bad, truth be told. People came to him when they had a magical problem—gremlins in the mill works or fairy lights in the pasture, potatoes that spoke in tongues when you baked them, or roosters that laid eggs that hatched into snakes and toads. Minor things.

Oliver would listen to the problem, or gingerly accept a handful of prophetic potatoes, nod gravely to the client, and go into his room in the attic. There he would pore through his books—usually the *Encyclopedia of Common Magic*—until he found what might possibly be causing it, and then, with trial and error and *101 Esoteric Home Remedies*, he would go out and try to fix it.

Either because he was so young, or because the old mage had been old for such a long time and they had gotten used to a fairly low standard in wizardry, the villagers were fairly understanding of his mistakes. It helped that he didn't charge until he was a hundred percent sure that the problem was gone, which usually meant waiting for at least a week and several follow-up visits. And he never charged very much anyway, which probably helped even more.

By the time he was eleven, Oliver was pretty good at identifying problems, if not always solving them. He could tell a possessed potato from one that had merely been planted in a patch of bad ground—magic lay under the dirt sometimes, like groundwater, and root vegetables were prone to draw it up—and he knew when to get out fire and salt and hemlock to drive out the wicked spirit at the heart of the spud, and when to simply advise the farmer to plant kale there in the future. He knew six charms to banish fairy lights (which one to use depended on the weather and it generally took at least two tries before he'd hit the correct one), and he could tell when a gremlin infestation was bad enough to merit a charm bundle made out of anise and quail bones, and when to just send in the cats.

Most of the charms and recipes required herbs, so he'd learned a certain amount of herb-lore, but it was tricky stuff, and he had to rely heavily on the armadillo's sense of smell. His mother, who was very proud of her son the wizard, planted the more common plants in her herb garden, or grew them in pots on the windowsill. But some things only grew out in the woods, or along streams, and he'd have to go looking. When roosters got a touch of cockatrice fever, and started laying eggs full of snakes, for example—you needed wood sorrel for that, and trout lily. That involved a hike through the woods with the armadillo trotting at his heels.

Oliver was stocky and tended to be on the plump side, but

scrambling around in the forest looking for obscure plants, his only guides a book of black-and-white drawings and a snide armadillo, had kept him reasonably fit.

Magic was hard and tricky and demanding, and it went wrong more often than not, but it was interesting, too, like solving a constantly changing jigsaw puzzle.

It was a pretty good job, all things considered. He hadn't learned many real spells—three in all, and the one to protect against armadillo dander probably didn't count—but he knew plenty of recipes for charms, and the villagers paid in eggs and cheese and butter and bacon, sometimes more than he and his mother and sister could eat. They had the best fed pigs in the village. The armadillo had eaten so much that he was reduced to a slow waddle and insisted on being carried everywhere, until Oliver put him on a strict diet of only one egg a week, and no more cream.

This worked until his sister had gotten married and moved away and now the eggs were starting to pile up again. But it would have been unforgivably rude not to accept food when people were determined to give you *something*, so his mother had been pickling eggs by the gallon. Some days it seemed like half the plants he gathered went to season pickles.

It was the plants that had alerted him to the drought.

He was used to plants by now. He knew the difference between the shapes of leaves, whether they were pointed like a spear or had fingers like a hand, whether they were fuzzy or waxy or smooth.

He knew that none of those leaves should be turning brown and curling up at the edges.

He knew that the bluebells should be sending up leaves like cabbages at the end of March, not the beginning of February. It got warm too early and the plants came up too early and then it got hotter and hotter and they died early, too. The trees budded out a month before the spring festival and their roots began to drink the wells dry.

Oliver knew that the streams should be choked with liver-cress right now, and that the edge of the forest should be thick and green, instead of brown and dry.

Instead, the streams were mostly mud and the livercress had vanished months ago, which meant that he was using dried leaves instead of fresh, and it worried him.

It worried him more when he walked through the marsh and found it dry and crackling underfoot, the grasses as stiff yellow as broom bristles. It looked like late fall instead of summer.

It was bad. Trees that he had known when he was barely old enough to toddle were losing leaves like they were going to die.

That was why, when the mob had showed up, they'd found him with his bag already packed.

Somebody had to bring back the rains, and apparently it was going to have to be him.

❁

Apple trees lined the edge of the road as they passed the orchard. The few apples that hung from the branches were small and tired looking. The drought hadn't done them any good, either.

They weren't ripe yet, but Oliver hadn't had any breakfast. The likeliest one of the lot was far out of reach.

He stopped, leaning against the fence rail. The armadillo took advantage of the halt to wash his face like a scaly cat.

"*Pushme, pullme...*" whispered Oliver under his breath, and concentrated hard on the stem of the apple.

Doing a spell was a hard thing to explain. It was like thinking hard about something, but sort of sideways. You concentrated, and you said the word, and then you *pushed* with the inside of your head, really hard—

The stem snapped, and the apple slipped through the leaves, bounced off a branch, and landed at the edge of the road. Oliver pounced on it.

He'd learned the *pushme pullme* spell the previous spring, when Harold the miller had a gremlin infestation in the mill and hadn't bothered to call him out until they started breaking the machinery. It was dangerous to have gremlins in the mill—if they got caught in the gears and ground up with the flour, the bread had a tendency to explode, or bleed, or turn into a flock of starlings and go screaming around the kitchen. But Harold had always been cheap, and he didn't care if people complained.

When faced with a potential repair bill, though, he'd called Oliver out quick enough, but by then, quail bones and anise and rue wasn't nearly enough. They'd left little packages of mischief meshed in all the gears and cogs, and Oliver had to go over the entire millworks, popping out each mischief and catching it in a clean linen handkerchief. He'd had a huge bag full of the stuff by the end, like a sack full of smoke and nettles. It had taken days, while Harold breathed down his neck and lost money, and Oliver had mastered the *pushme pullme* spell in desperation, to knock the mischief loose, or pull it close enough to grab.

It wasn't nearly as useful as having an invisible hand—he'd read about such a spell but couldn't get it to work—but it was about as good as having an invisible foot. You could close doors with it, or prop them open, pull things close or kick them away. If he was very patient, he could pick up fairly small things, with almost exactly the same painful mental effort as trying to pick something up with his toes.

It was also an excellent spell for picking apples he couldn't reach. He took a bite. It was sour but refreshing.

"You'll regret eating that later," said the armadillo.

"I know," said Oliver, taking another bite.

## 3

Oliver slept that night under a tree, which was horribly uncomfortable. He had a jacket for a blanket, and his backpack for a pillow. As pillows went, it did not compare well to his goosedown pillow at home. It was lumpy and buckled and the corner of *101 Esoteric Home Recipes* dug unpleasantly into his cheek.

The shortcomings of the pillow, however, were nothing compared to using the ground as a mattress. Things poked him and prodded him, the ground was hard and rocky, and the only crop to survive the drought seemed to be the bumper crop of insects.

His discomfort was made worse by the queasy, cramping feeling from eating not one but *three* sour apples. They had been delicious at the time, but it wasn't a good thing to eat on an empty stomach. He hadn't even bothered making dinner. (The armadillo hadn't said *I told you so*, which only made Oliver that much more aware that his familiar had indeed told him so.)

"Quit squirming," grumbled the armadillo.

"There's rocks on the ground," muttered Oliver.

"It's the ground. It's *made* of rocks."

Not for the first time, Oliver wondered if speech was really a good idea in a familiar.

After a minor eternity of something that wasn't quite as satisfying as sleep, but was at least a little like it, the sun came up. Oliver got up with it. He drank from the drainage ditch beside the road. There was a thin film of dust on top of the water. Insects clung to the dry plant stems and sang back and forth across the armadillo's head.

"Are we going to do that every night?" asked Oliver as he climbed out of the ditch. "Aren't there farm houses along the way or something?"

The armadillo stood up on his hind legs and scratched his belly. "I don't know. Nobody comes out this way, do they? This is all farmland... *was* all farmland... but I've never seen any of the farmers in town."

Oliver wondered if the farms had been abandoned. The fences weren't in great repair, it was true. He wondered if there'd be more weeds if there was more water to grow them. A few patches of soil, lying lower than the rest of the fields, were fuzzed with green, but no one had planted out crops. There was a hard crust on the ground. He didn't think it had been plowed this year. Maybe not for several years.

"All I know is that if we go far enough, then we get to Hark-hound Forest," the armadillo said. He dropped back down and gazed at the distant mountains. "It's the forest I'm worried about. It has a reputation."

"What sort of reputation?" asked Oliver.

"A bad one. And my mother said that the slugs tasted wrong."

"Oh, well..." Oliver knew the ultimate condemnation when he heard it. "How far is it?" He kicked himself mentally for not having asked earlier.

The armadillo considered. "Five or six days to the forest, I think."

"Six *days?*" Oliver already felt like he'd been walking forever. Sleeping on the ground for one night had been bad enough.

Sleeping on the ground for a half-dozen nights would probably leave his spine in a permanent kink.

"It'll take longer if we stand around talking," said the armadillo, plodding down the road on stumpy legs.

Oliver sighed. "Is there a shortcut?"

"Buy a horse."

They didn't have enough money for a horse. Oliver counted the coins in his purse and figured that they could afford maybe a hoof and a couple of hairs off the tail, if it wasn't a very good horse. There was also a distinct lack of people to buy horses from.

He rummaged in his pack and pulled out a biscuit. It had been fresh and crumbly yesterday. Today it was rather chewy, and it made him thirsty. He had to scramble back into the ditch and take another drink of the dusty water.

The armadillo continued to plod. Oliver ran wet hands through his hair and over his face and went after him.

⚅⚄⚅

It was a long day, and nothing happened during it, except that Oliver's feet hurt and his eyeballs ached from the dust and the glare. He shook out the cloth that had held the biscuits, soaked it down, and wrapped it around his forehead. That helped a little with the glare.

They walked and sometimes they stopped to rest. There was not much comfort to be had sitting in the dust on the side of the road, so they never rested for long. When the armadillo's short legs began to tire—not that he would ever say anything, but Oliver could tell—Oliver would pick him up and carry him.

"You've got biscuit crumbs in your hair," said the armadillo, and then there was the snuffly, ticklish sensation of a snout against his scalp. Oliver laughed involuntarily but let his familiar pick them out.

They saw no other humans. Occasionally there was a farmhouse standing empty. Once, far across a field, he saw something that might be a goat or a sheep, but it did not approach.

It occurred to Oliver that not only had he never gone any farther along this road than the orchard, he'd never really wondered what was out here. It hadn't been forbidden, and thus interesting, the way that the ruins of the old watchtower had been. It had been known among the children of Loosestrife that there was nothing much in this direction, so no one had bothered. You could stand on the edge of the orchard and see fields and fences and there was no reason to believe that there was anything different beyond them.

*Fat lot of good it would have done me if I had wondered, though. Even if I'd come this way on a whim, I'd have gotten bored long before I stopped for the night.*

Evening was starting to come on, and he was starting to wonder when to stop for the night—should he stop early, make a fire, and have one of the little packets of tea in his pack? He hadn't seen any place that looked more comfortable than last night's tree.

He almost didn't want to stop. Sleeping on the ground was nearly as exhausting as walking. Maybe if he walked all night, he'd actually be less tired in the morning.

Oliver suspected that the armadillo would tell him what a stupid idea that was, so he didn't say it out loud.

He was plodding along the line of a fence—one of an endless series of identical split-log fences, edging more or less identical fields—when he heard a bang.

He looked up, startled, and realized that it was the door on a farmhouse near the road. He'd been concentrating on his feet and not paying attention and hadn't even noticed the house. Hurrying down the wagon-track from the house was a tall, stoop-shouldered man.

The man didn't speak until he was at the road, and then he stood there and waited until Oliver had drawn closer.

"Boy," he said, which might have been a greeting or an observation. He had a very deep voice, and the hand on the fencepost nearest Oliver was enormous, with dark red knuckles.

Oliver decided to treat it as a greeting. He didn't recognize the farmer, but country hospitality, even in these times, meant that he might get a spot in the hayloft and a bite of dinner. "Hello, sir."

There was a long silence. Oliver waited politely, and then, when that didn't seem to be working, he said, "May I beg your hospitality for the night, sir?"

"Hospitality," said the farmer.

Oliver began to wonder if the man was touched in the head. Simple, maybe. Maybe he could only repeat what people said to him. He had dreadfully bad skin, not just pocked but with a strange, stretched look between the marks, and dark, deep-set eyes.

*Has he had the pox, maybe? I know it comes with fever sometimes, and a fever can damage the brain...* Learning herb-lore meant you picked up a little bit of medicine, even though Oliver wasn't a healer and would never pretend to be one.

The armadillo gave an odd little shake, settling his armored hide. The farmer looked down as if seeing him for the first time.

Most people would probably comment on the fact that someone had a pet armadillo, even if they didn't recognize a familiar when they saw one. The old farmer said nothing.

Oliver began to despair that there might be any dinner, but he held out hope that the hayloft might still be open. Hay was terrible on his allergies—the spell only worked on armadillo dander—but the ground was terrible on his back, so maybe if he alternated between the two, he'd survive long enough to get to the Rainblades.

"Might I sleep in your barn for the night, sir? I promise, I will disturb nothing."

"Barn," said the farmer again. "The barn. Oh, aye." He shook himself, rather like the armadillo, and his gaze seemed to sharpen. "And come to the house for thy supper."

*Thy?* Oliver thought. *Who says thy anymore? It's a writing word, not a speaking word...*

*It's supper*, said a rather more practical voice, and that decided him.

◌◌◌

The farmer's wife was named Mrs. Bryerly, which presumably made the farmer Mr. Bryerly, but Oliver was too busy eating to ask.

Well... trying to eat.

It was a strange meal. Nothing had been cooked. It was a sort of odd hodge-podge of preserves and ancient, crusty bread and a raw onion and half a wheel of cheese with moldy edges.

It wasn't the worst meal he'd ever had, but it was... well, an odd thing to set out for a visitor. Oliver supposed that they'd eaten earlier in the day and Mrs. Bryerly hadn't wanted to cook a whole meal for a passing stranger, but it did resemble a bunch of things dragged at random out of the pantry without much thought as to how they went together. Cheese and bread and onion you could just about see, but blueberry preserves? And he had no idea what was supposed to be in the other jar at all, except that it was brown and gritty-looking.

A bit of the cheese wrapped in a bit of the onion and plastered on a hunk of the bread was edible, if awfully dry. Oliver had to ask for water, and there was a long pause and then Mrs. Bryerly jumped up and said, "How silly of me! Of course!" and shooed Mr. Bryerly off to the pump to fetch some.

Even if his throat hadn't been dry from the bread, Oliver doubted he could get a word in edgewise. Mrs. Bryerly was as tall as her husband and much wider, but she still managed to *flutter* somehow, in a manner that might have been girlish once but now resembled an injured goose trying to escape the farmer. And she talked non-stop. Oliver had barely managed to tell his story, and only in the vaguest terms before she ran over the top of it with boundless sympathy.

"So hard!" she said, for the third or fourth time. "To send a boy all that way!" She dabbed at her eyes. "So cruel! So inhuman of them!"

Oliver stared at the cheese, feeling strange.

Here was somebody ready to agree with him on every count, and instead he had a strong desire to defend the villagers, because... well... they *weren't* inhuman. Not at all. Vezzo was a good man and always brought around a cut of beef after slaughter, and Matty had lost two children and had a fragile sweetness that would shiver into tears if you said an unkind word to her.

"Such unfeeling brutes! Oh, you poor boy!"

Sure, they'd done a pretty mean thing, putting him on the road like that, Harold had certainly been awful about it, but... well... he *was* the wizard. Somebody had to bring rain. And they'd been scared. Scared people did cruel and stupid things, sometimes, but Vezzo and Matty had still done their best for him.

"Oh, if I could only give them a piece of my mind! I would!"

Oliver found himself missing his mother. Not that you could admit that, not if you were a twelve-year-old boy—you might as well just give up completely at that point. But her no-nonsense briskness would have been a welcome counterpoint to Mrs. Brylery's fluttering. He poked at the brown preserves with a knife, wondering what they were and how they would taste on bread.

"Still thy tongue, wife," rumbled the old farmer.

"Oh, dear," she said, ignoring her husband, "oh, dear. It seems so hard! If only he could stay with us!"

Oliver opened his mouth to say that it was fine, he was the wizard and this was his job, but closed it again instead.

The farmer was watching him, and something—his archaic speech or the deep hollows under his eyes or something else

Oliver couldn't quite put a name to—made the young wizard feel desperately uncomfortable.

It wasn't a rational thing, it was certainly rude, but he suddenly wanted nothing so much as to bolt from the room, away from the fluttering of Mrs. Bryerly and the strange, glittering eyes of her husband.

"If—if I could just stay in your hayloft tonight—" he stammered. It seemed this dreadful dinner could not be over soon enough. He bit into the preserve-covered bread. Fig. He hated figs. He tried to swallow, nearly choked, and had to take several large gulps of water.

"Oh, no! Oh, poor boy, you must stay here with us. We'll make you up a bed by the fire, all nice and snug." She beamed at him, ignoring the fact that there was no fire, that the hearth was cold and cobwebbed and clearly had not held a fire for a long time. The only light came from the windows, which had faded until he was very nearly eating in the dark.

"No! Err—" Oliver didn't question why or how, but he *knew* he didn't want to stay in the house. "Ah—I can't. It's my familiar. He—err—he's not very well housebroken."

He expected a tail smack for that, but the armadillo was sitting bolt upright at his feet and didn't so much as flick his ears.

Mrs. Bryerly's nose wrinkled. "Oh," she said, in a rather less fluttery voice. "Oh, I see."

There was an awkward silence. Mrs. Bryerly's hands flexed, twisting the edges of her apron. She also had enormous knuckles, like red walnuts.

"I'll see thee to the barn, then," said Mr. Bryerly, and rose. Oliver jumped up and followed.

The farmyard's shadows lay deep and indistinct in the twilight. Oliver followed the stoop-shouldered form of the farmer across the yard. The ground had been churned to muck by years of hooves, and then dried into an irregular, treacherous landscape. Shrubs shielded the house in leafy darkness.

"Mind thee don't scare the cows," said the farmer, lifting the heavy wooden bar from the barn door. He held the door open. "Hayloft's down at the end."

"Er. Thank you," said Oliver, stepping into the barn. He glanced around. It was very dark, except for a few chinks where a little light slipped in. "Ah, is there a—"

Creeaaaaaak.

The door shut behind him. Darkness slapped him across the face.

"Err—"

He heard the thump as the bar was ground into place.

Oliver did not like this at all.

"Armadillo, can you—"

The tail smacked across his shins. He fell silent.

A minute or two dragged by. Oliver heard the grunt of something alive from farther down the barn.

"Arma—"

The armadillo gave him another warning tail flick.

Oliver waited. Something big was breathing in the dark.

Then he heard it, without quite realizing what he'd been listening for—the sound of the farmer's footsteps, going away.

Mr. Bryerly had stood outside the barn for several minutes, not moving.

That was... well, it was awfully creepy, anyway.

"He's gone," said the armadillo quietly, after the footsteps had faded. "We're locked in, though."

"Well," said Oliver doubtfully, "I suppose you still have to lock the barn so the cows don't get out..."

"There are no cows," said the armadillo grimly. "There's two pigs, and they're scared to death."

"We're strangers."

"They're not scared of *us*."

"Oh."

Silence fell. Oliver waited for his eyes to adjust to the darkness. He could hear the armadillo scuffling around.

"Why would he lie about the cows?"

He half expected the armadillo to snap at him, but instead, he came over, and Oliver felt the small, scaled weight lean against his legs. "That's an interesting question," said the armadillo. "I don't think he meant to, actually. I think he either forgot there were no more cows, or it was something he thought he was supposed to say, without quite knowing what it meant."

"What kind of farmer forgets about his cows?" asked Oliver, baffled.

"One that isn't really a farmer, I expect."

This was not comforting.

"Do you think they're imposters?"

"I think they smell sweet," said the armadillo unexpectedly.

"Huh?"

"*Sweet.*" The armadillo's tail flicked like a nervous cat. "Like maple syrup and ant eggs, both of them."

Oliver considered asking when the armadillo had sampled maple syrup and ant eggs and decided that perhaps he didn't want to know.

"Not a normal smell, anyway," the familiar continued. "Maybe not a human smell."

This was even less comforting.

"You think they're not human?"

"Does it matter?" The armadillo shrugged, making a kind of armored ripple. "Either they're inhuman monsters pretending to be a sweet old couple, or they're a sweet old couple that's planning to kill you and bury you under the barn."

"Good lord!"

*Buried under the barn?* he thought, and then, exasperated at himself, *Does it really matter where they intend to bury you?*

A grunt came from the darkness. Oliver saw a snout push into a patch of moonlight, and a gleam of small black eyes.

"Can you—err—talk to the pigs? Maybe they know what the Bryerlys are."

"Hmm. Maybe. Pigs are pretty smart. There are some excellent pig familiars."

"Eww. Who'd want a pig for a familiar?"

It was too dark to see the armadillo's expression, but the outline of his ears had a wry tilt. "I don't know... if you were, oh, just hypothetically, say, *locked in a barn by a couple of murderers,* would you rather have a ten-pound armadillo or our four-hundred-pound friend with the tusks over there?"

"Oh." Oliver considered this. "I think I'd still rather have you."

"Hmph." Despite the circumstances, he could tell the armadillo was pleased. The familiar pressed briefly against his shins, then stumped over to the pig pen.

Watching animals communicate was not particularly interesting. They mostly stood around, shifting on their feet, and breathing. Now and then one of the pigs would grunt. If there was anything more exciting going on, it was lost in the shadows.

Oliver sat down on a crate and concentrated on listening to the sounds outside. He thought he might be able to keep the doors shut with the *pushme pullme* spell, if Mr. Bryerly came back, but probably not for very long. And of course, the doors opened out, so he couldn't brace them shut from this side.

Eventually, one of the pigs stamped its foot and squealed. They both looked in the direction of the farmhouse. The armadillo sighed and also looked towards the farmhouse.

This seemed to end the conversation. The pigs retreated to the far corner, standing tightly packed together, and the armadillo drifted back over to where Oliver was sitting.

"I hate talking to pigs," he muttered. "It takes weeks to get the kinks out of my tail..."

"What did they say?"

"They didn't *say* anything," grumbled the armadillo. "They're not people in pig suits. They don't have a language like 'Swinese' or something. They're *pigs.*"

Oliver waited patiently. The armadillo tended to rant when he was nervous.

"They're scared. It smells like they've been scared for a while. There used to be more pigs, and I think something bad happened to them."

"What happened?"

"I don't know! They can't tell me. They can't really describe things, okay? Pig vocabulary is basically 'yes/no, food, fear, happy, this-pig/not this-pig.' There's not a lot to work with." The armadillo sighed. "But whatever happened, it was bad, and it scared them, and I get the feeling it wasn't just like a pig being slaughtered. It seems like it must have been something weird."

"Do they have names?" Oliver asked, rather interested. Communication with another species, even a pig, was something none of his books covered, and the armadillo didn't quite count.

"Do they have—yes, they're called Bacon and Pork Chop." The armadillo hopped in frustration. "Of course they don't have names! They're *pigs!*"

"Oh."

After a minute the armadillo relented. "They know who they are," he said. "They know the difference between this-pig and that-pig. But they don't have names like you and me. They don't need them."

This was fascinating and Oliver stored it away for later, but it was not particularly helpful at the moment.

"We have to get out of here," he said. "I mean, obviously. I'd say we should wait until the Bryerlys are asleep, but they might be waiting until we're asleep."

"Mmm. Yes." The armadillo considered for a moment. "We have to take the pigs."

"What? With us?"

"No, no, but we have to let them out."

"Where will they go?"

A shrug rippled against his leg. "I don't know. The woods, probably. Anywhere. We can't leave them here."

"But—feral pigs—" Oliver had seen dogs torn up by pigs gone feral, and he didn't want to see it ever again. A wild pig was as dangerous an animal as they ever saw around Loosestrife, worse than bears or mountain lions.

Still, the armadillo was right. They really couldn't just leave them with the Bryerlys.

"Can you get them to promise not to hurt anybody?"

The armadillo scoffed. "No more than you could. It's not that they wouldn't, it's that there's no real way to communicate the concept. Pigs don't make promises."

"Oh." Oliver sighed. It wasn't much of a choice, really. "Well, I guess there's no help for it. We can't just leave them here. So, let's get out, then."

This was easier said than done.

"How *do* we get out?" he asked. The enormity of the situation clutched at him. "I'm only a minor mage," he said, mostly to the pigs, feeling the need to apologize even though they couldn't understand him. "I can't call down lightning or make an earthquake or call up spirits to go after the Brylerlys."

He paused as the idea hit him. "Well, I suppose I could try to call up an elemental—"

"We're in enough trouble without you bleeding from the nose," said the armadillo.

"I'm sorry—"

The tail that smacked his ankles felt like a whip. "Ow!"

"Quit apologizing! It's not going to help!"

"Sor—oh, hell." He tried to work out a way to apologize for apologizing and gave up.

"When you're done," said the armadillo, "you can get over here and see if that spell of yours will lift the bar."

"Oh. Oh!"

Having something useful he could do, even if it wasn't calling down lightning, made Oliver feel a lot better. He crouched by the barn door. Warping over the years had left a small gap between the doors—not enough to fit a finger through, but just enough to see the plank barring the door.

It was a very large, very heavy plank. Knots twisted through the grain like rippling muscles.

"I've never moved anything this size before," he confessed. "I don't know if I can."

"Only one way to find out," said the armadillo, plopping himself down on Oliver's feet.

Oliver nodded. He fixed his gaze on the plank, murmured *"Pushme, pullme..."* and concentrated.

The plank rattled against the fastenings, but didn't move.

Oliver gritted his teeth and pushed harder. He could feel his blood pounding inside his head. He had to lift at least one end of the plank up and over the metal hook holding it.

It was a lot heavier than anything he'd ever tried to move before. It felt like the plank was inside his head, a big, immovable object between his eyes. The bar jumped in its fastenings and landed again with a thump.

"Unnnngghhh..."

The far end of the plank started to rise.

"Unggh...!"

*Something* gave. Whether it was in the wood or inside his head, he wasn't sure. There was a loud mental *pop!* and the spell snapped.

Oliver sat down hard and clutched his temples.

The armadillo gave him a brief, friendly poke with its nose, then trotted away to shove its head through one of the chinks in the wall. It was back a moment later.

"You got the bar lifted, but it turned in the socket. It's hung up on the fastener. Can you try again?"

"I don't think that would be a good idea," said Oliver. His brain felt swollen, like a raw red sponge inside his skull. It didn't hurt, but it didn't hurt in a way that indicated a whole lot of hurt lurking underneath. "I think I broke something."

The armadillo eyed him for a moment. "Hmm. You don't look so good. The blood leaking from the corners of your eyes doesn't help."

Oliver moaned. This was worse than the time with the elemental.

"Maybe we can just push it," his familiar said, putting his shoulder against the door.

Since the strength of an armadillo is negligible, Oliver staggered to his feet and braced his shoulder against the door. It creaked, but held fast. He pushed harder, feeling the pulse start up in his head again, and heard the bar grinding in the socket.

"Easy, now," said the armadillo, patting his knee with a small paw. "You're brains, not brawn. Sit down and rest a minute."

"If we wait, the Bryerlys might come out," said Oliver weakly, although he wanted very much to sit down and rest.

"We won't wait. Sit down."

Oliver sagged to the floor. The books in his pack dug into his back, but he was too tired to rearrange them.

The armadillo trotted across the dusty boards to the pigpen. He scrambled awkwardly up the fence—armadillos are not noted for their climbing skills—and flipped the latch with his nose. The gate creaked open.

"You're letting the pigs out now?"

"Relax," said the armadillo.

*Easy for him to say*, thought Oliver. The black-and-white sow was bigger than he was, and the boar, an immense dirty white pig with tusks like fence posts, was nearly twice that. He hugged his knees nervously.

The armadillo walked briskly up to the boar, without showing the least fear, and pushed the pig's leg with his nose. The pig looked down at him. The armadillo scampered away, three or four lengths, then turned and looked over his shoulder at the pig, jerking his snout towards the door.

It was hard to read emotion on those faces, particularly in the dim light, but Oliver could swear the boar looked baffled.

The armadillo repeated the gestures—snout touch, run, look back. The boar scuffed his hoof on the floor thoughtfully. The armadillo tried again.

Oliver's familiar was gearing up for the fourth try when the black-and-white sow lumbered out of the corner, grunted irritably at the boar, and followed the armadillo to the gate of the pen.

"Right," said the armadillo. He scooted under the fence and pushed the gate partway open. The sow got her head around it and shoved it the rest of the way.

They crossed the floor, the sheepish boar bringing up the rear. Oliver discovered that he did, indeed, have the strength to get up and get out of their way.

Once they reached the door, the armadillo approached the sow. He pushed her leg with his snout, jerked his head at the door, then shoved himself against it, legs scrabbling for purchase. It creaked slightly.

The sow grunted thoughtfully and pawed at the ground. She went up to the door, put her shoulder against it, and began to push.

The wood groaned. She grunted at the boar, who took up a position at the other door and began to push. The armadillo got out of the way, sitting up on his hind legs to watch.

Wood splintered. The boar started to drop back, but the sow grunted irritably at him, and he threw himself into it again.

There was a sudden, painfully loud screech of metal—Oliver cringed—and the doors swung open.

Jumping forward, Oliver saw that the wood had held, but the screws hadn't. The pigs had ripped the metal hooks right out of the wood.

"They'll have heard that!" said the armadillo. "Run for it!"

The pigs needed no urging. As soon as the doors opened, they bolted across the yard.

A shout went up from the farmhouse. Oliver saw a lantern swinging wildly, throwing a spray of light across the broken ground, and had the useless thought that it was the first light he'd seen the farmers use.

Oliver sprinted around the corner of the barn, into the safety of the shadows, his weariness forgotten. He raced for the edge of the barn, in the direction of the road—and halted.

The fields were bare, the stunted crops only knee high. There was no cover anywhere from the barn to the road, unless he could reach the drainage ditch, which would be so obvious that the Bryerlys were sure to check it. If he ran for the road, he'd stand out like a horse in a pigpen, and then it would be a footrace.

With his skull still throbbing like a shattered star, he wasn't sure how well he'd be able to *walk* the distance, never mind running.

There was only one place to hide, one place they might not check.

He had to hide close by the farmhouse. The thick shrubs would provide cover until the Bryerlys gave up looking. Then he could sneak away before dawn.

He knew it was the logical hiding place, but his stomach roiled at the thought.

Squeals of rage came from the yard, with a hoarse yell of pain. Mr. Bryerly had apparently tried to grab one of the pigs.

Oliver ran along the back side of the barn, towards the house.

He peered around the corner of the barn and saw the farmer's back. Mr. Bryerly was limping after the racing pigs, the lantern held high.

Oliver winced, biting his lip, but there was no help for it. He scurried across the open space, bent nearly double, waiting for a shout of alarm.

It didn't come. He could have wept with relief, but he didn't dare stop. He ran crouched, staying low, until the farmhouse loomed in front of him.

Distant squeals indicated that Mr. Bryerly was probably still occupied. Oliver hoped the pigs would get away safely.

The chimney side of the cottage was the farthest from any doors, and the most thickly overgrown. An ancient lilac bush had nearly eaten a corner of the cottage. It was long since out of flower, but the leaves made a dense screen of dappled light and shadow in the moonlight.

"Good enough," said Oliver under his breath. He looked around and saw no one. He ran the three steps across the yard and dove into the lilac bush.

Twigs yanked at his hair and poked for his eyes. He wiggled deeper, until his back was pressed against the fieldstone wall of the cottage, in the deep shadow of the fireplace.

The wall was cold and lumpy. He was sitting on rocks that felt like they were the size of potatoes, and there was a twig poking him in the ear.

*Is this enough? I can't get any farther in.*

Lilac leaves made a shifting curtain. He could only see the yard in tiny, moving glimpses. He hoped that would be enough.

He hoped that he was really as invisible as he thought, and that his feet weren't sticking out.

He hoped the armadillo was okay.

The twig poked him in the ear again.

A splash of light appeared at the edge of his vision. Mr. Bryerly trudged across the yard. Oliver breathed through his mouth, silently, his knuckles white on the strap of his pack.

If the farmer saw him, he'd have to bolt out of the lilac and make a run for it. He had his last spell, his third spell, which might buy him a little time, but probably not nearly enough.

Tying somebody's shoelaces together with magic had seemed incredibly funny when he was six. Now it just seemed like a waste of magic.

*Oh lord, why couldn't I have been one of those kids who set things on fire?*

It wasn't that he particularly *wanted* to have been a disturbed six-year-old, but being able to set the Bryerlys on fire would have been so much more *useful*.

Light came through the leaves, turning them briefly to green stained glass. Oliver squeezed his eyes shut to prevent the shine from giving him away.

The twig went for his ear again.

Mr. Bryerly paused a few feet away. Oliver didn't dare open his eyes. He could see the light redly through his eyelids.

*If I hear the footsteps coming here, I'll run. No, no, it could be a coincidence, he could be walking past, and I'd be an idiot. If he says something, I'll run. If I hear the footsteps, and he says something—but what if he doesn't say anything?*

He suspected that if the farmer stood there long enough, the pounding of his heart would give him away.

"Not back here," said the farmer, and Oliver started. The voice was wrong. Instead of the deep, archaic speech, Bryerly's voice was thin and waspish. "Gone to road."

"Well, go after him!" said Mrs. Bryerly. Oliver started again. Her voice had no flutter to it at all now, but that wasn't the problem—from the sound of it, she was standing directly in front of the lilac. He hadn't heard her approach.

He sneaked a glance through slitted eyelids. Sure enough, a deep shadow stood in front of the bush, hands on hips. Fortunately, she seemed to be facing away from him.

It occurred to him that she was probably blocking him from the farmer's view, entirely by accident.

"After. After?" The lantern swung as Mr. Bryerly made an expansive gesture. "Do you see... see..." A long pause, as if remembering words. "Gone. Not seeing. Not on road."

"Where's the smell go?"

"Smell?" Mr. Bryerly made a thin squealing sound of frustration. Not a human sound. Oliver sank his teeth into his lower lip. "All I smell is pig and leg. Too much blood. Makes me... hungry..."

"Useless! Are you just going to let him get away?"

"Let him? Not letting! I'm not letting! Do you see him? Gone."

Mrs. Bryerly made a noise that Oliver had never heard come from a human throat, a sort of gurgling growl, like a hungry wolf at the end of a long drain. He pressed himself silently backwards, trying to wedge himself into the stone wall.

The end of the twig had gotten lodged in one of the fleshy folds on the rim of his ear and was now gouging in earnest.

"Should have... should have made him sleep..." grumbled Mr. Bryerly.

"Fool!" snapped Mrs. Bryerly. "Drug a wizard with his familiar watching? It would have known, and then we'd be in a pretty pickle."

"Gone now. Pigs gone, too." Bryerly grunted. "Long wait until next one. Long... hungry... wait..."

"Wait? Do you really want a mouthful of wormwood, then? The wizard'll tell everybody, and they'll be down here faster than you can skin a hog."

In his hiding place under the lilac, Oliver's heart clenched like a fist.

Do you really want a mouthful of wormwood, then?

The *Encyclopedia of Common Magic* was prodding his back, but he didn't need to open it. He could see the page in his mind's eye, the neat black text, the small, careful ink drawing beside it.


Ghul—Also called Ghouls, Draugs, and Corpseaters. These cannibalistic creatures may once have been human, but no one is quite sure how a ghul is created. The bite of a ghul does not seem to transmit the curse, but those who live among ghuls often become ghuls themselves, which has proved a limiting factor on research.

The ghul can masquerade quite convincingly as human, for short periods, but this seems to require effort, and the illusion is rarely perfect. They usually have large, red-knuckled hands, odd skin, and sometimes pointed teeth, and of course, an insatiable craving for human flesh.

A ghul can recover from quite horrific injuries, but can be killed by traditional methods (fire, drowning, dismemberment) or by wormwood, thrown in the mouth, which destroys it near instantly.

The Bryerlys were ghuls.

*I am an idiot*, Oliver thought, clutching his forehead. *I should have seen that. Her knuckles were huge, and his skin was awful. They must have been eating the pigs when they couldn't get people. And they wouldn't light a fire bigger than that tiny lantern.*

They'd been too scared of him, a wizard, to attack directly. Oliver would have laughed, if it wasn't so absurd. If they *had* attacked, he might have tied one's shoelaces together for a few seconds, and then what? Throw the armadillo at them?

He was a very minor mage. He had never felt more minor than at that moment, trapped under a bush while monsters argued less than five feet away.

He wished his mother was here. He had never appreciated his mother enough. She'd have yanked down the sword she kept over the door and chopped the ghuls into little bits.

He'd even have been glad to see his sister. She lacked his mother's skill for physical mayhem, but she'd have had the pigs lined up in military formation and marching on the farmhouse.

The twig was boring a hole in his ear. At this rate, if he ever got back home, he'd be able to wear an earring the size of a saucer.

"What do we eat, then?" asked Mr. Bryerly the ghul. There was a distinctly whiny note to his voice. "Got no pigs and no boy and not even that scaled rat familiar. What do we *eat?*"

"You, if you don't shut up!" snapped Mrs. Bryerly. "Wrap up that leg or I'll take a bite out of it myself!"

"But—"

The shadow in front of the lilac moved. There was a loud *crack!* of flesh on flesh. Mr. Bryerly whimpered.

"Shut up!" railed the ghul. "We'll think of something." She turned and stomped away.

"Didn't need to hit me..." muttered the other ghul resentfully. He followed, feet dragging. The light went with him, and left Oliver in darkness.

He exhaled. He knew he couldn't have been holding his breath the whole time, but it felt like it.

He heard the footsteps fade, the cottage door slam. Muffled voices came from inside, then fell silent.

And that was all.

Oliver reached up and yanked the twig out of his ear.

He had to wait to cross the fields for at least a few more minutes. He was getting very cold, but he couldn't make too much noise. He had to wait until he was sure the Bryerlys weren't going to come back out looking.

As unobtrusively as possible, he rearranged his pack so the books weren't jabbing into his back. Every creak of cloth and leather sounded like cannon fire in his ears, but no one came running.

He had to wait.

He really had to wait.

He wondered how long he'd been waiting.

Fear was bad, fear and boredom together were practically unbearable. He tried counting breaths, heartbeats, lilac leaves, and stars. He wondered if it had possibly been long enough. It felt like hours had passed, but the moon hadn't budged at all in the sky.

Something poked his thigh. Oliver choked back a scream, but a thin squeak emerged anyway.

It was the armadillo. His familiar froze, ears swiveling, but nothing stirred in the cottage.

"You made it..." breathed Oliver, so quietly that he could barely hear himself.

The armadillo nodded. He looked around, then grabbed Oliver's pant leg in his teeth and tugged. Oliver leaned forward, and the armadillo dropped the fabric and jerked his head towards the road.

Oliver nodded. *I may be a very minor mage, but at least I'm quicker on the uptake than the pig.*

He crawled out from under the lilac, raced across the yard, and over the stone fence. The armadillo came after, scrambling up and over the wall and down onto Oliver's back like a stepladder.

They hurried along the wall, down to the barn again. On the far side, with the barn between them and the house, Oliver paused.

"Come on!" whispered the armadillo. "If they really are farmers, they'll be up at dawn!"

"They're not farmers," said Oliver. "They're ghuls. I don't think they'll be up at dawn."

The armadillo paused. "Ghuls?" He scuffed his paws in the dirt. "I didn't think—not here—are you sure?"

"They talked about eating me, and about mouthfuls of wormwood."

"Ghuls. Well. That explains it. They'll eat livestock if they can't get humans. Let's move."

Oliver felt very exposed as they left the shadow of the barn. The barn would only block the farmhouse's view for a few hundred yards. Long before they reached the road, they were hurrying along under the baleful gaze of those dark windows. If the ghuls looked out, they would be seen.

The skin on his back crawled.

"We're fine," said the armadillo quietly. "No one's coming."

"Sorry," said Oliver. "I just—"

"I know." The armadillo paused in its trotting long enough to push reassuringly against his calf. "You did good. Hiding by the house was a good idea—they checked the barn pretty closely.

When they didn't see you on the road, the man thought you'd gone invisible."

"I *wish*." Invisibility was an immensely difficult spell. Oliver couldn't read half the words of the introduction, let alone the spell itself. "Did the pigs get away?"

"I think so. The boar took a chunk out of Mr. Bryerly's leg. Assuming it formerly *was* someone named Mr. Bryerly, and not some random ghul pretending to be him."

"I think it probably was just pretending," said Oliver. He looked over his shoulder again. "He couldn't remember the cows. I think any farmer would remember how many cows he had, even if he'd become a ghul."

"Hmm," said the armadillo. "You're probably right."

Oliver swallowed. "What do you think happened to the real Bryerlys, then?"

"Best not to think about it. Here's the ditch."

They reached the drainage ditch at the road. Oliver slid down the weed-choked slope. There hadn't been any rain for months, but the bottom was still thick with green stems.

He reached the bottom and sat down hard.

"We should keep going," the armadillo said.

"I know," said Oliver thickly. "I'm sorry. I'll get up in just a minute."

"Mmm." The armadillo came and sat on his feet.

It was being safe, even in the dubious safety of the drainage ditch. It didn't make sense, but now that he wasn't in so much danger, all the fear came plunging out of the back of his brain and ran away with him. His breath caught in his throat.

Oliver couldn't burst into tears—not with the ghuls so close, even if they couldn't hear him—but he felt a few tears slide, thin and hot, down his face. He felt very much like a child, not at all like someone who had braved a pair of bloodthirsty ghuls.

He'd been so sure, back in the village, that he could do this. He'd been worried about bringing extra *socks,* as if that mattered at all in a world with man-eating monsters in it.

He'd been so annoyed at the villagers, not for making him go, but for not being properly grateful about the fact that he was planning to do it *anyway*.

*I can't do this*, he thought bleakly. *That's why Mom wouldn't have let me go. She'd have known what it would be like.*

He was barely two days down the road. How could he possibly get to the Rainblades? He was too minor a mage. The armadillo had saved him, and the pigs, but next time there might not be pigs, or the enemy might not be so foolish.

He wrapped his arms around his head and wished for his mother, which only made him feel younger and more hopeless. A real wizard wouldn't be huddled in a ditch wishing for his mother.

(In this, at least, Oliver was dead wrong—many wizards over the ages, some of them very major mages indeed, have found themselves curled in ditches and wishing desperately for their mothers. But they tend not to mention these things in their memoirs.)

The armadillo leaned against him. Oliver reached out blindly and rubbed his familiar behind the ears. The gesture was so normal, so much like what they did every day, that it helped steady him. His next breath didn't catch quite so hard in his throat, and he scrubbed at his face with his sleeve and wiped tears and blood away.

Maybe he couldn't go all the way to the Rainblades. Maybe it was a fool's journey after all.

But now, at this moment, he could get up.

"Okay," he said, crawling to his feet. "Okay, let's go."

۞

The next few hours were very strange.

The drainage ditch was about five feet deep and the weeds that grew up the sides rose another ten inches in the air, so Oliver could walk along the bottom without ducking down to stay out of sight. The moon was sinking but the air had the strange brightness of a midsummer night, and the bottom of the ditch was thick but not overgrown, full of horsetails and yarrow rather than brambles. So, his footing was not difficult to find— he only had to keep putting one foot in front of the other and keep his eyes on the small form of the armadillo trotting ahead of him. Sometimes his familiar was lost in the shadows, but the grass stems moved around him, a white froth of flowers churning in his wake, and Oliver was able to keep pace.

This was good, because the young mage was nearly asleep on his feet.

It had been a long day, and a much longer, more frightening night. His head had stopped pounding, but there was a dull pressure on it, as if his brain was swollen and pressing against the insides of his skull.

After the first hour or so, he wasn't really awake. It was more like being in some long dream of walking, a dream woven together of the hiss of leaves against his pant legs, the soft footsteps of the armadillo, the distant calls of night birds and the hypnotic thrumming of crickets. It did not seem like a thing that could really be happening. It was a dream, surely. There was no ditch, no plants, no distant ghuls. There was no armadillo, no person called Oliver. Surely, he was somewhere else, someone else, and this was only a dream, a brief fantasy of a very minor mage.

Later on, he thought it was most like the time when he was eight and had a raging fever. Too tired to stay awake, too miserable to really sleep, he had sunk into a long waking dream that wavered across the line of hallucination. The cottage and the bed and everything he thought of as *Oliver* had gone away. What was left of him hung suspended in a strange, indistinct world where he froze and burned and froze and burned.

It had been a long time before the fever had broken.

This was a little like that. He walked and dreamed, neither asleep nor awake. He thought for a while that the ghuls were

walking next to him—it seemed that they must be, somehow—
but when he roused a little and looked to either side, there were
only the sides of the ditch. A little while later, he looked for his
mother the same way, but the dream of her shredded into leaf
and stem and dried grasses.

He didn't know how long he had been walking. Perhaps he
had always been walking. Perhaps everyone else in the world had
died of old age, and he was still walking.

The bottom of the drainage ditch developed a distinct slope.
Oliver listed sideways and caught himself. The heavy jar of his
foot on rocks roused him a little from his dream.

"Whuh—? Hnnn?"

"Here," said the armadillo. "Up here."

The ditch had run into a stream. A low bridge crossed the
road. Oliver stumbled toward it.

"Ghuls...?" he said. He wasn't sure what the word meant
anymore, only that it was important.

"Lie here," said the armadillo, herding him with his tail and
one paw. "Under the bridge, just past these plants."

The plants were silvery-gray and had small, ridged leaves on
long stems. Blue flowers rose in long spires, washed pale by
moonlight. When Oliver struggled through the stand, a heavy,
dusty smell washed around him.

"Catmint," said Oliver, to himself or the plants or the
armadillo.

"It'll hide your scent. Come on."

Oliver went to his knees. The shock of his palms hitting the
dirt seemed to take a long time to travel up his arms and down
his spine. "I'm tired," he said to the armadillo.

"You should go to sleep."

Oliver needed no more urging than that. He slept.

A few hours before dawn, the armadillo lay in the catmint stand, watching the road. Moonlight lay over the fields and turned the road into a ribbon of bone.

A figure came running down it. It was shaped like a man, but it did not run like one. Its arms were held straight down by its sides, the knuckles large and red, fingers scissoring at it ran.

The armadillo did not move, did not blink. He might have been a collection of slick stones. Only his eyes moved, imperceptibly, following the ghul's path as it ran.

The ghul did not even pause at the bridge. The heavy smell of catmint hung in the night air, eclipsing the smell of a small boy, or the faint, leathery scent of armadillo. It crossed the bridge, footsteps thumping, and continued on.

Oliver, dead to the world, did not even wake as the ghul passed. Nor did he wake, just before dawn, when the ghul thumped back the other way, hurrying now, afraid to be caught out on the road by daylight.

The armadillo had always been glad that Oliver didn't snore. His life had just never depended on it before.

He waited until the dust had settled from the ghul's passing, and then carefully extended a paw and nibbled thoughtfully at his claws.

The countryside needed rain. The drought had gotten bad, if ghuls were coming out and devouring farmers and going unnoticed.

He had considered leading Oliver around in a wide circle, back to Wishinghall and his mother. The Rainblades were no place for a child, even a mage.

But the drought needed to be broken. Things were worse than he had realized. It seemed unlikely that Oliver would be the one to do it, but perhaps all mages were unlikely. Somebody needed to try.

The sun came up, hot and pitiless. Dust shimmered in the light. The armadillo sighed and got to his feet.

"Come on," he said, nudging Oliver with his nose. "Time to go."

I t was another long hot day. The sky was mercilessly blue. Grasshoppers sang in the ditch. There should have been frogs calling, too, but Oliver had only heard one, creaking out a "hnagh-hnagh-hnaaaagh," like a broken door hinge. It sounded lonely.

"Well," said Oliver, trudging along, "at least we got away from the ghuls."

He said it out loud, partly to hear his own voice over the grasshoppers, partly in hopes that the armadillo would agree with him. Hearing about the ghul crossing the bridge in the night had made him queasy, more ill than terrified.

The armadillo didn't say anything.

"Surely they won't follow us," Oliver tried. "They've got their spot on the farm, they won't risk leaving it..."

The armadillo still didn't say anything. His tail left a long snaking line in the dust.

"Armadillo?"

The familiar stopped and turned his head, meeting Oliver's eyes.

"Oh god," said Oliver, feeling his stomach clench, "they're following us, aren't they?"

"I don't know," said the armadillo. "But I think they will. With the pigs gone, there's nothing left to eat on the farm, and you know about them and might raise the alarm. There are lots of reasons to come after you, and very few not to."

"Should we get off the road? Try to hide?"

"Not yet." The armadillo faced forward again and began stumping along on his short legs. "We're more likely to run into people on the road. They probably won't attack a group. And they won't start moving until evening. They don't pass well in daylight."

Oliver bit his lip.

"Besides," said the armadillo, picking up the pace, "this is the only road to the Rainblades that I know about. If we leave it, we risk getting lost."

"What if we don't find people before tonight?" asked Oliver.

"We'll sleep off the road a little way. No fire tonight."

"There's hardly any food to cook anyway," said Oliver glumly, and followed the armadillo down the road.

By noon, Oliver had made a discovery. If he held his copy of *Encyclopedia of Common Magic* in front of himself, and looked up every few seconds, the road was flat enough and straight enough that he could read and walk at the same time.

He read the entry on ghuls five or six times, as if hoping that more information was lurking in it somewhere, and if he read the article often enough, it would spring into existence on the page.

It failed to materialize. *Stupid book.*

What good was such a short article? Why didn't it tell you what you really needed to know, like how far a ghul would follow you, or if they were attached to their home territories? The entry for unicorns was twice as long, and what good was that to anybody? Unicorns were cowards and only dangerous in packs. Every now and then you'd get one hanging around the village trash heap, but it'd run off if you yelled at it. But there it was, six whole paragraphs, and meanwhile he knew no more about ghuls than he had an hour ago.

Oliver sighed. They had come to another bridge. The armadillo scrambled down the embankment to the water and Oliver tucked the book under his arm and followed him.

The water was warm and dusty, but better than nothing. Oliver filled his waterskin again.

This time, rather than going over the useless entry for ghuls, Oliver looked for spells. What he'd really needed last night was to be invisible, even if just for a short time. There was a spell for that. It was complicated, but he had nothing else to do right now.

"Hexus," he read, under his breath. "Hexus el-ashin invisio..."

"What's that?" asked the armadillo sharply, turning his head. "What are you up to?"

"I'm trying to turn invisible," said Oliver. "If I could get the invisibility spell to work, I wouldn't have had to run from the ghuls."

The armadillo snorted. "You can't cast that one."

"How do you know?" asked Oliver. "I bet I could. It's fern spores and magic words, which is pretty straightforward. I can get the spores in the forest. Then I'll have them, and if the ghuls show up—"

The armadillo shook his head. "The old mage couldn't cast that one at the height of his powers. You're wasting your time."

Oliver gritted his teeth. "I can learn the words."

"You can learn the words," agreed the armadillo, "but you don't have the power. Not yet. Maybe when you're older."

*Maybe when you're older.* Oliver fumed silently. He wished people would make up their minds. He was too young to learn powerful spells, but apparently, he was old enough to send off on his own to bring rain back from the other side of a cursed forest.

"It's not fair," he growled.

"What is?" asked the armadillo. "Look, there are other spells.

They're smaller, but they might be useful. You could find one to cover your smell. Or to make yourself look like a tree, say."

"Oh, that's useful," muttered Oliver. "I'm running away from the ghuls, and hey, presto, a sudden tree in the road! They'd have to be pretty dense not to see through that."

The armadillo snorted.

"I'm tired of being a minor mage," said Oliver.

"Minor isn't useless," said the armadillo. "Remember the Jenson kid?"

Oliver bit his lip. The Jenson kid had been seven years old and had been trying to climb trees. He'd picked one covered in poison ivy and hadn't realized it. He'd rubbed his eyes and wiped his nose and when the rash came on, both eyes swelled shut and his nose closed and all he could do was lie in bed and sob miserably, while his mother held his hands down to keep him tearing his own skin off.

Fixing poison ivy wasn't hard. Oliver had come right away and done the cantrip with the herbs. He'd done it twice, just in case, and sure enough, in under an hour, the swelling went down and the kid could open his eyes and breathe again. His mother had thrown her arms around Oliver and nearly cried. Mrs. Jenson was a tall, raw-boned woman, and she'd put her face down on top of Oliver's head and kissed his hair. Oliver had been both touched by her gratitude and desperately uncomfortable. That much emotion made him feel like he was seeing inside people's guts, and he didn't want to know so much about them.

Obviously, he was glad that he'd been able to help with such a small thing. He fixed poison ivy all the time, and he didn't ever charge for it because he wouldn't have wished that kind of itching on his worst enemy. But he'd much rather have been able to turn invisible or throw lightning around. Something impressive that didn't leave people hugging you and crying.

They kept walking. Oliver tried to fix the invisibility spell words into his memory anyway. The armadillo was younger than he was, and he wasn't right about everything.

49

## 5

I t did not take as long to reach Harkhound Forest as the armadillo had thought. Perhaps his mother had remembered the journey incorrectly, or perhaps the forest had crept toward them. They were only four days out from the village when a band of darker blue appeared on the horizon.

The armadillo lifted a paw and pointed. "Harkhound," he said.

"It looks big," said Oliver, eyeing the sweep of dark blue. It went as far as he could see to the south, and most of the way to the north. The white peaks of the Rainblades, which were visible from the village on a clear day, seemed to float over the backs of the trees.

"It *is* big." The armadillo started walking again. "I'll be glad to get there," he said over his shoulder.

"Will there be food, do you think?" They were down to extremely scant rations. Oliver had been scavenging what he could from the ditches, but the drought had left food scarce. He'd been chewing on sorrel awhile, which had a pleasantly sour taste, but you'd get sick if you ate too much.

He'd been hoping that there would be farmhouses, but there weren't—or more accurately, there *were*, but they were empty.

It was unsettling. The ground was dry and cracked, but that was only from this summer, wasn't it? It shouldn't have been enough for people to *leave*. He knew farmers, he'd grown up with them, and they felt about the land the way wizards felt about their familiars. It was the land that told them what they were.

The fields lay fallow. There was a short stubble of weeds in places, and in others the ground was bare. The farmhouses looked like hollowed out jack-o-lanterns, with the windows and doors gaping open.

"Did something happen here?" asked Oliver. "We'd have heard about a plague, wouldn't we?"

"Would we?" asked the armadillo. He paused and sat back on his haunches. "Nobody goes to the Rainblades and Harkhound, do they?"

Oliver thought about it. Everyone said that the Rainblades were strange and dangerous, which was why sending a mage was such a big deal. And now that he thought about it, everyone from Loosestrife went north and east and south, but not very far west. There was the little belt of orchard and woods and then some farm fields, but he couldn't think of many farmers that lived more than a day's travel to the west.

"I guess not," he admitted. He felt annoyed with himself for never noticing before, and never asking what lay to the west. He'd just assumed that it would be farmland of the sort he understood.

*That's such a little kid thing to think. I should have done better. I'm a mage, even if I'm only twelve.*

They kept walking and passed more buildings. There was something that might have been a barn, but it had collapsed. Some of the houses looked as if they had been abandoned for a long, long time.

"Should we go in one?" he asked. "I mean... there might be food."

"Might be ghuls, too," said the armadillo, trotting along. "Or worse things than ghuls."

"*Are* there worse things than ghuls?"

The armadillo threw a brief, ironic look over his shoulder at Oliver. "You've read that book of yours. Aren't there?"

"Yeah..." admitted Oliver. "I just didn't think they'd be... you know... *here*."

That was also the way that a child would think, and he knew it. He walked along with his head down, feeling his stomach growl.

He'd nicked a few cabbage leaves growing alongside the road. He felt a little guilty about it, even though it was obviously wild and going to seed. The farmhouse off in the distance was missing a roof and most of an upper story, so it wasn't like anyone would miss it.

Cabbage wasn't exactly stealing. If they passed a living farm with corn or eggplant, though, he wouldn't be able to help himself, and that *would* be stealing.

*If we pass a living farm, I can pay for food, though. And maybe they can explain what happened here.*

"Once we get to Harkhound, we'll be able to get off the road," said the armadillo.


"Off the main road?" Oliver was surprised. The road had become his whole world over the last four days, circumscribed by split rail fences and drainage ditches. "Why? I thought you said we'd get lost?"

"We might," said the armadillo. "But something's definitely following us."

"What?" Oliver twisted his head to look behind him and saw only the slowly settling road dust. His stomach churned. The sorrel leaf suddenly didn't taste so good. "The ghuls?"

"Most likely," said the armadillo. "I haven't seen them since the first night, but I'm nearly certain. I'd hoped we'd meet more people, so I thought we should stay on the road as long as we could, and it's not like there's a great deal of cover in these fields anyway, but..."

He trailed off. Oliver nodded glumly. The road had been deserted. And they certainly weren't likely to meet anyone in Harkhound Forest, which meant that if the ghuls were coming after them, they were on their own.

He went back to reading about invisibility. When he looked up again, the blue band on the horizon had gotten almost imperceptibly larger.

❦

They reached the forest edge around noon. The contrast could not have been more stark. On one side, fallow fields baked in the sun. On the other, the forest cast leafy shadows across the road.

The wagon ruts had vanished from the road a few miles back, at the last farmhouse. The broad road became narrower and fuzzed with green, but not completely overgrown. Even here, the drought had reached brown tendrils. Dried seedheads clicked together along the road, and the crickets sang a parched song. But there was green under the trees. The leaves were wilted, but not dry and curled.

The dirt under Oliver's feet was packed hard, and vegetation hadn't colonized it at all.

"It's an old roadbed," said the armadillo, when Oliver scuffed at it with his toe. "There was a time when people travelled to the Rainblades regularly."

"What stopped them?" asked Oliver.

The armadillo gave him a thoughtful look. "Now that is a very good question, isn't it?"

"And I'm guessing you don't know the answer?"

"No," said the armadillo. He stepped under the shade of the trees. Leaf shadow dropped bits of dappled light across his armored back. "Perhaps we'll find out."

One thing was certain, Oliver thought a few minutes later. Harkhound Forest felt *alive*.

There had been birds in the fields, perched on thistle stems in the ditches, singing occasionally from fence posts. But there were a great many more in the forest. Oliver saw them as much as heard them—little brown creepers scurrying up tree trunks and nuthatches with striped heads scurrying down. High up in the canopy, vireos sang their monotonous tune: *Here-I-am where-are-you, here-I-am where-are-you.*

The path became a mat of pine needles, edged in liverworts. A great vine of poison ivy snaked up a tree beside the path, its stem covered in roots like a centipede's legs, and Oliver scooted to the far side to keep from brushing against it. (He could fix poison ivy—mostly—with herbs and a couple of magic words, like he had with the Jenson kid, but it was a pain and he didn't have all the herbs with him.)

A burbling sound off in the distance indicated a stream. Oliver's head jerked up when he recognized it. To have water—clean, flowing water, not something from a ditch—seemed a sudden luxury. He would love to wash his hands, and maybe even his clothes. He'd been wearing the same pants since he left the village, and they were so stiff with dust and sweat that there was a cracking sound when he bent his knees.

The armadillo made for the stream without asking. They had to step off the path, but any qualms Oliver felt—ghuls or no ghuls—were immediately washed away by the sight of the water.

It was a picture-perfect forest stream, the water dark and dappled, whipped to silver as it crossed the rocks. Oliver dropped his pack on the leafy shore. "Is it safe?" he asked, licking his lips.

The armadillo raised his head and sniffed. "No strange spirits. Of course, there's *him.*"

Oliver followed the line of his familiar's nose and let out a squawk.

The young man sitting on the rock looked as startled as Oliver felt.

For one thing, he hadn't expected to see anybody out here, particularly not in the ill-omened Harkhound Forest, and if he *had* expected to see anybody, it wouldn't have been a scruffy dark-skinned teenager with a growth of scraggly beard and acne scars on his forehead, carrying an ancient and mangled lute.

For another thing, the young man was a mage.

He wasn't much of one, Oliver was pretty sure, probably not even as much as Oliver himself, but one of the things you picked up along the way was an ability to tell magic in somebody else. There was a hint of color around them, a thread of brightness to their outline. Oliver's master had called it an aura. His had been very bright indeed. The young man's wasn't much at all, but still—

"You're a wizard!" said Oliver.

"I'm *not*," said the young man wretchedly. "Not really."

The armadillo slapped Oliver's shin with his tail and muttered something about manners.

"Sorry," said Oliver contritely. "I—uh—I didn't expect to see anyone out here. Um. Hi. I'm Oliver."

He stuck out a hand. The young man looked at it gloomily and then stuck out his own. "I'm Trebastion."

"That's an odd name," said Oliver.

"I know," said Trebastion morosely. He looked around. "Um. Pull up a rock, I guess. There are plenty." He bent his head over the lute and began plucking at it—*plunk! plunk!*—like drops of water into an out-of-tune puddle.

"Thanks," Oliver sat down on a nearby rock, trying to find a position that didn't involve something digging into his buttocks. The armadillo jumped in his lap like a cat, which didn't help matters.

"Your familiar?" asked Trebastion. Oliver nodded. Trebastion went back to his lute: *Plunk!*

"So..." said Oliver, when it became clear that Trebastion wasn't going to say anything. "What are you doing in the forest?"

"I could ask you the same thing," said the young man. "Actually, I probably *should* ask you, because you're an awfully young kid to be wandering through a horrible forest alone with only an armadillo, even if you are a wizard. But I'm not going to. It's none of my business. I assume you're running away from something."

"Actually, no, I—"

PLUNK!

"It's none of my business," said Trebastion firmly. "I don't want to know. If there's an angry master coming after you, the less I know about it, the better."

The armadillo snickered.

"There's nobody after me," said Oliver, surprised. "Well, I mean, there might be some gh—"

*"None of my business!"* (Plunka-plunka-PLINK!)

Oliver considered this. "Is somebody after *you?"*

Trebastion snorted. "Probably. They always think it'll be a good idea, and then of course it isn't, and I get blamed, even though I always warn them." He gave a particularly hostile tweak of the strings, and something twanged warningly near the neck of the lute.

"Er?" said Oliver, who wasn't following this at all.

"The important thing," said Trebastion, plucking the lute as savagely as a cook might pluck a chicken, "the really *important* thing is that there's nobody out *here.*"

Oliver was of the opinion that if there had been anybody in the immediate vicinity, they would have left with their hands over their ears. The lute was dreadfully out of tune, but it didn't seem to matter, since Trebastion couldn't play a tune anyway.

He was just wondering if he could ask Trebastion to stop when one of the lute strings broke. Trebastion yelped and sucked on a finger.

The armadillo sighed with relief.

"So... um... you came out here to get away from people?" asked Oliver, gesturing awkwardly at the looming woods. This seemed a little extreme, rather like jumping down a well because you were thirsty.

"People!" said Trebastion. "Always wanting things. Well, I'm sure *you* know. You're a wizard."

"Oh yes," said Oliver. "In fact, my village sent me out to—"

"None of my business," said Trebastion hastily. He glared at the broken lute and swung it off his lap. "You want some lunch?"

Oliver tried not to drool. He had eaten the last of his food yesterday, which had been dry and stale and mixed with lint from the bottom of his pack. "If you have any, I'd... um... it would be very nice."

Whatever Oliver might think of his playing, Trebastion was not stingy with his food. He had bread and cheese, which he broke exactly in half, and handed half to Oliver.

"Thank you," said the very minor mage, torn between wanting Trebastion to know how grateful he was and not wanting to look pathetic in front of the older boy.

Trebastion shrugged. "You looked hungry. I've been hungry. Happens a lot. Usually when I'm between one village and the next." He stared broodingly at the lute.

There didn't seem to be much to say to that. Oliver slipped the armadillo a bit of cheese and scooped up a cupful of stream water. It tasted exactly like he'd thought it would—cold, clear, with a faint tang of soil and leaf.

"Are you a minstrel, then?" Traveling minstrels came through town a few times a year. They were generally considered an entertaining nuisance, but even the worst of them could play a lot better than Trebastion.

Trebastion grumbled into his cheese. Oliver decided not to ask any more questions. The young man might possibly be crazy, but he *had* shared his lunch, and Oliver didn't want to make him mad.

Truth be told, he didn't want Trebastion to leave. He hadn't realized how badly he'd been craving another human voice. It wasn't that the armadillo didn't count, it was just... well...

"Suppose I can tell you," Trebastion said, licking crumbs out of his palm. "You're practically a colleague, after all."

"I am? Uh... sure?" Oliver looked down at the armadillo. The armadillo shrugged.

"Being a wizard."

"Oh, that."

"I make harps," said Trebastion morosely. "Fiddles, too."

"Oh?"

"Out of bones."

"Oh."

Trebastion seemed to be waiting for something. Oliver cast about for something to say. "I didn't know you could make harps out of bones."

"You can't. That's the magic bit." He sounded both unhappy and rather proud. "They shouldn't play at all, particularly not when you string them with the victim's hair and all. No tensile strength to hair."

Oliver put a foot down on the rock and eased himself into a position where he could bolt as soon as he got a chance.

"Not *my* victims," said Trebastion, exasperated. "I don't *have* any victims. Wouldn't know what to do with one."

"That's good," said Oliver faintly.

"It's just... look, I was walking along by the mill one day back home, and there was this poor drowned woman who'd washed up there. I mean, she'd washed up a while ago, and the fish had been at her, so there really wasn't a lot left but bones and some rags and hair, and I—I looked down at the bones and I just had this *compulsion*, and the next thing I know, I'm rooting around inside a corpse—"

Oliver felt slightly queasy and fed the crust of his bread to the armadillo.

"It was *horrible*," said Trebastion. "I mean, can you *imagine?*"

Oliver could, rather more vividly than he wanted to.

"Anyway, the next thing I knew I was assembling this... harp. It looked like a harp, mostly. More than it looked like anything else, anyway."

Oliver nodded. He'd had that happen with the vegetables sometimes when the magic got into a field—they weren't quite vegetables anymore, but they were more like vegetables than anything else. Brussels sprouts were the worst. They actually grew fingernails.

"It was mostly magic holding it together," Trebastion continued, "and then when it was finally done—I couldn't stop working on it, you understand, it just—I had to finish it—and then I put it down, and the awful thing started *playing*."

He looked at Oliver, apparently expecting surprise. Oliver looked at him blankly. It was a magic harp, what did he expect it to do? Cook omelets?

Finally, he said, "What did it play?"

"Murder ballads, mostly," said Trebastion gloomily. "That one got stuck on *Oh the Dreadful Wind and Rain*. Sometimes they do others. But that's not the worst bit. They shriek."

"Shrieking is bad," agreed Oliver.

"They won't shut up, either. They're murder victims, you see —I can only make the bone harp when they're murdered—and then when their murderer is in the room, they scream like anything."

"Well, that could be useful..."

"Not as much as you'd think," said Trebastion. "I mean, yeah, it brings people to justice, but then they've got this screaming harp, and the things don't shut up. And what do you do with it? Hardly anybody can bring themselves to bury one while it's still screaming, and cremation is right out. They don't seem to care if their murderer gets locked up or hung or anything, they just keep screaming. It's pretty awful."

"It *sounds* awful."

Trebastion folded his arms. "So here I am, trying to get away from all... that." He waved a hand vaguely behind him. "The last town was pretty bad. It was twins, and the harps did this awful harmonic line with each other, and even though their aunt *asked* me to do it... yeesh. I was not popular." He gazed morosely at his lute.

Oliver had no idea what to say to all of this. Fortunately, Trebastion didn't seem to expect him to say anything.

He felt tired and sweaty. He pulled off his shirt and swished it back and forth in the stream.

Trebastion watched this without comment. After awhile, he reached into his pack and dug out a bar of soap, which he tossed to Oliver.

"Thanks," said Oliver.

Trebastion shrugged one shoulder. "I've learned a few things about wandering between towns. Soap's worth packing."

"I'll remember that," said Oliver. "Although if I ever get back from the Rainblades, I don't want to wander ever again." He realized that he was speaking the absolute truth. Even Harold the miller's red face would have been welcome right now. It would have meant he wasn't so far from home.

"Rainblades, huh?" asked Trebastion. "I'm not asking why you're going there, you understand."

"It's really not a secret..."

"Not asking!" Trebastion waved his hands. "But do you know if they have harps?"

"Uh..." Oliver looked at the armadillo.

"Musical instruments wasn't one of the things my mother thought to mention," said the armadillo.

Apparently Trebastion knew enough about familiars not to be surprised by a talking armadillo. "Huh." He hunched himself up on the rock. His cuffs were too short at both the wrists and the ankles, as if he'd been growing out of his clothes. "Do you think they have murder victims?"

"Um." Oliver scrubbed the soap into the armpits of the shirt until he'd worked up some suds. "I suppose every place does eventually, don't they?"

"You're a cynical kid," said Trebastion.

"You make harps out of *dead people*," said Oliver.

"Yes, but I haven't allowed it to taint my basic optimism."

The armadillo snorted. Oliver wrung out his shirt and tried smacking it on a rock a few times. It made a satisfying wet *thwack!*

"Tell you what," said Trebastion, "I'll come with you."

Oliver stopped thwacking. "What?"

"To the Rainblades." Trebastion picked up his lute. "They may be just the audience I'm after for my musical talents."

Oliver suspected that the only audience for Trebastion's musical talents would be stone deaf, but wasn't sure how to say this tactfully. He was using the older boy's soap, after all, and Trebastion *had* shared his bread and cheese.

He wasn't sure how he felt about having Trebastion come with him. He didn't seem like a bad sort, but he did make harps out of murder victims.

On the other hand, that probably wasn't his fault. Magic took people that way sometimes. There were people who didn't want to be wizards, wouldn't know the first thing about how to become wizards, but it turned out they had some bizarre wild talent for something specific.

Oliver's mom had told him about a friend she'd had when she was young, who charmed chickens. Chickens would leave whatever they were doing and mob her. She didn't particularly want chickens, she didn't like them, but they would peck through stone walls to be near her.

Eventually she'd had to run away to sea, where there were very few chickens.

Oliver had always thought that was a terrible wild talent to have, but it really didn't compare to being compelled to make harps out of murder victims.

It sounded very unpleasant, mostly for Trebastion.

And if the ghuls were after them, it might be nice to have another set of eyes and ears.

Then again, it was *also* possible that Trebastion could be a terrible person who would kill a boy and his armadillo in their sleep, or worse yet, force them to listen to his music.

Still...

The armadillo cleared his throat. "You should know," he said, "even if you don't come with us, that we had a run-in with some ghuls a few days ago."

"Ghuls?" said Trebastion. "Corpse-eaters? Like in the stories? Seriously?"

"Big knuckles, bad skin, the whole lot," said Oliver. "Along with the cannibalism, of course."

"Huh." The musician looked over his shoulder. "You're sure?"

"Oh, very. They wanted to eat us."

"There's a chance they may have followed us to Harkhound," said the armadillo.

Trebastion thought this over while Oliver wrung his shirt out a few more times. It was still very damp, and putting it back on felt disgusting, but it was a warm day and it would dry out soon enough. If he tried to cram it in his pack, it'd probably get all moldy and he'd still have to wear it eventually.

"So, there may be ghuls in the forest."

"Right," said the armadillo.

"But you guys are going to try to go *away* from the ghuls." Trebastion said slowly.

"That's the plan," said Oliver.

"Then I'm definitely coming with you." He rubbed the back of his neck. "Actually... well, fair's fair. There may be a few people after me, too."

Oliver waited.

Trebastion fiddled with his pack straps. "The last town... I said I wasn't very popular."

"You did," agreed Oliver.

"Yeah, well... turns out the murderer *was*. Popular, that is. Regular pillar of the community. Everybody was very upset.

There were some very unkind things said. As if I could *make* a harp accuse the wrong person."

Oliver put a hand over his eyes and felt very old.

"So. Err. His relatives were very angry. They may have broken him out of the holding cell. I mean, it wasn't much of a cell, it was the church cellar, that's not much a cell if you ask me, particularly not for somebody with fifty relatives, half of them church elders, but—well, anyway." He fiddled with the pack straps some more.

"So, this guy's relatives are still mad at you?"

"I left town in a hurry," said Trebastion. "But I think they might be. There was a lot of yelling. I didn't stick around to see who it was directed at. If they weren't after me then, they might be *now*, anyhow—the harps never shut up, you understand, and I'd be the convenient scapegoat, and they might think that killing me would make the harps stop shrieking."

"Would it?" asked Oliver, professionally interested. Some magics did persist after the wizard died, while others stopped immediately, and there was no real consensus on the topic.

"It's never been tried," said Trebastion. "I'm not real keen on finding out, you understand."

"So, there's a murderer after you," said Oliver.

"Yes, but there's cannibal ghuls after *you*," said Trebastion.

Oliver was forced to admit that this was fair.

"In that case," said the armadillo, stepping on Oliver's foot, "I think we'd be happy to have you travel with us as far as the Rainblades. We can watch each other's backs."

"Sounds delightful," said Trebastion, picking up his pack.

The armadillo strode confidently off into the underbrush, with the teenage musician in his wake, and left Oliver trying to catch up, wondering what exactly had just happened.

## 🎵 6 🎵

Travelling with Trebastion was better. Oliver was willing to admit that after the first hour.

It wasn't that he talked a lot, because he really didn't. The minstrel was perfectly happy to talk, but if Oliver or the armadillo stopped responding in more than monosyllables, Trebastion took the hint.

And it wasn't that he was good in the woods, because he wasn't.

"Is this berry edible, do you think?"

"No," said Oliver.

"How about this one?"

"Well, yes, I suppose—"

Trebastion popped it into his mouth.

"—but you'd have to be really desperate," Oliver finished, as Trebastion gagged and spit it out again. "Sorry, I didn't think you'd—well. That's bitterberry. You can use it as a spice, but it's not something you can really eat straight."

"Bleaaagghgh!" said Trebastion, gargling with stream water. "You should have warned me."

"I was *going* to..."

"Fair enough. I guess."

No, the really nice thing about Trebastion was the noises.

Every time a branch had broken, when travelling alone, Oliver had immediately thought, *It's the ghuls!* and turned to look. He did this even knowing that ghuls don't travel very far even in twilight, let alone in broad daylight, because while his head knew this, his gut was convinced that this one time, he had found amazing daylight-loving ghuls and *they were just about to eat him.*

It was not restful. In a forest filled with squirrels and birds and rabbits and other things that might make leaves rustle or twigs crack, it was the exact *opposite* of restful.

But since Trebastion was there, blundering along with all the woodcraft of a milch-cow, Oliver stopped worrying. If a twig snapped, it was probably Trebastion. If leaves clattered, Trebastion had probably stepped on them. If someone began screaming, "Aaaaah! Get it off me!" it meant that Trebastion had walked into a spiderweb again.

Having an explanation for the sounds helped enormously, even if every ghul for ten miles could probably have followed the sounds of Trebastion yelping.

"You're not used to the woods, are you?" asked Oliver, after a couple of hours of this.

"Not really, no," admitted the older boy. "Usually when I travel, I stick to the main roads. I'm very good at going to the back door of an inn and looking starved and pitiful and willing to wash dishes. There's a certain sort of woman who always wants to feed me. It's a survival skill."

"Huh," said Oliver. They had located a stand of huckleberries just coming into the late-summer fruit. The tiny, tart berries were delicious, but the thought of inn cooking—real cooking, with baked bread and roast drippings—was almost too much to bear.

"You're good at all this nature stuff, though," said Trebastion, waving a vague hand at the surrounding forest. "You know all the plants and stuff."

Oliver flushed. "I guess. It's from being a mage. You use a lot of plants, so you have to learn them. I'm not very good, though. I only know a few edible mushrooms, but I don't know the ones here and I'm not comfortable guessing. There's probably lots all around us, except we won't be able to tell them from the really poisonous ones."

"I am hungry," said Trebastion, "but I vote that we avoid the mushrooms. I don't want to turn blue or explode or—err—"

"Vomit to death," said the armadillo helpfully.

"Thank you, yes."

They made camp that night in stages. When it was still light, they built a small fire and boiled water for tea. Dinner was the remains of Trebastion's cheese, sorrel leaves, a few slightly squashed huckleberries, and a peeled and roasted cattail root, which tasted like a potato crossed with a muddy rope.

"You're sure this won't kill us?" asked Trebastion.

"Pretty sure." The fibers were so thick that Oliver had to scrape them through his teeth. "It beats starving, anyway."

"If you say so," muttered the minstrel, tackling another hunk of cattail.

Once they had eaten and put out the fire, the armadillo got them back on their feet and struck out into the woods. "We've been going parallel to the main road," he said. "Now we're going to go due south away from it, or as close as we can manage. The ghuls might find the fire, but they won't find us, and we can backtrack to the road in the morning."

"Uh," said Trebastion. "That sounds... logical?"

"Are you sure we can find our way back?" asked Oliver, who knew a little more about how deceptive directions can be in the woods.

"No," said the armadillo. "But we can hardly miss the Rainblades, even if we do lose the road."

"I guess that's true." They plodded into the leaf-strewn woods.

"Where did you come from, anyway?" asked Oliver. "The last town, I mean. I didn't see any towns on the way here."

"North," said Trebastion. "I'm not asking where you're from—"

"Loosestrife."

Trebastion sighed. "See, I wasn't asking."

"It's not a secret," said Oliver, baffled. "I don't care if you know where I'm from."

"You're not running away from a cruel master?"

"Uh... no? I'm going to the Rainblades to get rain."

Trebastion was silent, except for the crunching of twigs. "Well, that's a thing you could do, I guess. Anyway, the last town was north of Harkhound. I went south along the edge for a bit, but there wasn't any place to hide except in the forest. And I know the forest is supposed to be weird, but it was better than getting caught by Stern and his buddies."

"Weird how?" asked Oliver. "I keep hearing it's bad, but not *how.*"

He didn't mind the forest. It was deeper than the woods he was used to, and the green was a darker green, but it felt alive in a way that the dead farms hadn't.

Trebastion shrugged. "I dunno. Stories. Strange lights. Trees walking around except they might be dead people, not really trees. The usual."

"I haven't seen any of that," said Oliver.

"The slugs taste normal so far," volunteered the armadillo, "but we're not very far in yet."

Trebastion gave this statement the grave consideration it deserved, and then fell down a hillside and had to be picked back up again.

"And there's the song, too," he added, slapping pine needles off his clothes.

"Song?" said Oliver warily.

Trebastion swung his lute around front and tried to strum a chord. It didn't go well for the chord. "Ah... let me see... there's a couple versions..."

"There always are," said the armadillo grimly.

Trebastion ignored this and launched into a song which, it became immediately clear, he did not remember.

"'Twas all late on a midsummer's day,
The farmer's wife, she lost her way,
In the trees, in the trees
The shadows lie deep
In the trees, in the trees
Where... uh... something sleep...
Something—uh—dark-haired wife
The farmer he vowed... oh, blast..."

He had a surprisingly deep singing voice, much better than his lute playing. His memory, however, left something to be desired.

"Look, I mostly do love songs," he said. "This one's not popular. People don't like to be reminded much."

"But what happened? Who lost their way?"

"The farmer's dark-haired wife," said Trebastion. "Depending on the version, either she got lost in the woods picking hazelnuts, or she ran away from him. So, he decides to burn the edge of the woods down in revenge, on either the trees or his wife. *In the trees, in the trees...* That's the chorus. I don't have the voice for it. You really need somebody who can do spooky and ethereal."

"But what happened to the farmer?" asked Oliver.

"Oh, he died," said Trebastion. He slung the lute back over his shoulder and hurried to catch up to the armadillo. "The woods burned, for *seven days and seven more*,"—he sang the words—"and the smoke that came out hung over the farms by the woods and killed everything. *The smoke, it lay as thick as sorrow, on the plow and on the harrow...* oh, hmm, maybe it wasn't *plow*, maybe it was *ground...*"

"Plow would make more sense," said the armadillo without looking back. "Speaking of agricultural implements."

"Sense has nothing to do with songs," said Trebastion. "What kind of idiot burns the woods down when somebody's lost in them? What if she had a broken leg? He'd have burned her alive." He shook his head. "Anyhow, that's supposed to be why the farms around here are all abandoned. The smoke from the woods poisoned the ground."

Oliver remembered the strange, empty farmhouses and the abandoned fields. "Did this actually happen?"

"Dunno," admitted Trebastion. They came to a small clearing and skirted the edge of it warily. "People say it did. I've heard the song performed and the old men at the bar say it was true and happened when they were a lad. But they'll say that about all kinds of songs. All I know is that once you get around the northeast corner of Harkhound, the farms are suddenly standing empty and there aren't any inns. You gotta go east for days to find even a little pothole of a town."

Oliver, who lived in that particular pothole, kicked himself again mentally for never having asked about what lay west. Why had he never asked? Why had nobody ever talked about it?

Because it was just farms and then the Rainblades. Because there was nothing worth seeing and the farmers came to us. Because things that have been empty since old men were lads just aren't very interesting.

And then he remembered Vezzo saying, "There's bad ground between here and there."

Of course, that's what the farmers would remember. Bad ground.

"But the trees didn't burn, did they?" he asked abruptly.

"Eh?" said Trebastion, who was trying to eat a pine cone.

"If this happened, oh—sixty or seventy years ago, say—we wouldn't have some of these trees. Forests come back fast, but some of these trees are hundreds of years old."

"Oh," said Trebastion. "Well, that's the end bit of the song. Most of the forest didn't burn. It just got angry. The smoke poured out over the fields and supposedly went on for miles.

*Fourscore leagues and ten,* I think, or *tenscore leagues and four,* although that'd be a really long way, so probably the first one. The farmer died in the smoke and all the farms were abandoned because it poisoned the ground, but the forest survived." He cleared his throat and sang:

"In the trees, in the trees
    Her spirit still walks
    In her kirtle of red
    In the trees, in the trees, in the trees."

"The farmer's wife, you mean?" asked Oliver.

"Yep," said Trebastion. "The forest was still there. Is still there. And her ghost is still wandering around it."

You would have to be an expert in armadillo body language (as Oliver was) to see the armadillo's skepticism. His familiar did not have much use for ghost stories.

"Why would she *want* to wander around it, anyway?" asked Oliver.

"Song doesn't say," said Trebastion. "But I figure she's mad at getting burned alive."

"Or at having married an arsonist," said the armadillo dryly.

"Well. That, too."

They walked along in silence for a little while. Oliver stubbed his toe and gritted his teeth. Trebastion fell over a stick.

"How persistent are the ghuls likely to be, anyway?" asked Trebastion, when he had gotten up again.

"I guess they'll follow us until they find someone easier to eat," said Oliver, who had been thinking about this subject a great deal for several days. "All the farms were empty. Maybe it was like your song, but I don't know for sure. And if there's no livestock and no people, I guess we're the easiest."

"Huh."

They kept walking. The shape of the armadillo started to grow fuzzy in the evening gloom.

"How persistent is *your* guy likely to be?" asked Oliver.

"Oh, fairly persistent, I imagine. He was the mayor."

"And he was *killing* people?"

"Believe me, I was as surprised as you are."

Oliver ducked under a branch. Trebastion didn't and yelped as it hit him in the face.

"So, you're after the rains," he said, when he'd stopped the bleeding.

"That's the plan," said Oliver.

"And the rain's in the mountains?"

"Supposedly the Cloud Herders have it," said Oliver. He didn't know what the Cloud Herders would be like, but he had a vague image of mystical priests, standing atop stone outcroppings while lightning played around their arms. Someone like the old wizard, with a long beard and robes, although with better hygiene and less underwear on their head.

Trebastion considered this for a while.

"Not very sporting, sending out a kid off to the mountains alone, is it?"

"I'm not that much younger than you," said Oliver, irritated.

"Yes, but the only thing people ask me to do is make a screaming harp, and it's not really *dangerous.*"

Oliver sighed. "They didn't know there would be ghuls," he said. He didn't know why he was defending the villagers, but he couldn't very well let Trebastion think they were all monsters. "And they didn't really mean to send me off the way they did. They were scared, that's all."

The armadillo said nothing.

"I'm scared," said Trebastion. "All the time. At the moment, I'm scared that Mayor Stern is going to come along and gut me like a fish. I still don't make people go off and get me rain."

Oliver rolled his eyes. "Yeah, but there's only one of you."

Trebastion tripped over a tree root. "I am sure that made a

lot of sense," he said, when he had recovered, "but I don't follow."

Oliver paused. The armadillo lifted his head and sniffed the air.

"You're one person," said Oliver. "And I'm one person. But there were thirty or forty villagers." He tried to come up with a good way to phrase it, to make Trebastion understand. "And they were all together, getting riled up and making it hard for each other to think. None of them would have done anything like that by themselves, except maybe Harold."

They continued on for a few minutes in silence, or as much silence as Trebastion could muster.

"But they *did* do it," observed Trebastion finally. "I mean, it happened."

Oliver sighed. "Yeah. But I'm not doing it for all of them *together* like that. I'm doing it for all of them *separately*. For Vezzo and Matty and... everybody. Our neighbors." He could picture them each distinctly in his head. Matty was probably crying over the chickens right now. Vezzo might even be looking off to the west, his big hands clenched at his sides, wondering if Oliver was okay.

"Seems complicated," said Trebastion.

Oliver shrugged. After a moment he said, "Do you know cows?"

"I have met a cow or two in my time," Trebastion allowed. "Horns. Udders. That sort of thing."

"Well, they're just cows, you know. They're important to the people who own them, but they're just... cows. But then you get a whole bunch together and sometimes they'll panic and stampede and run you down. They don't mean to hurt you, they're just scared. But they're still important to the people who own them. You don't just give up on cows all together."

"Yes, but you're still *dead*," said Trebastion. "Once they've trampled you."

Oliver sighed. "Yeah." He'd thought the cow analogy might

help Trebastion to understand, but maybe Trebastion understood perfectly well. "Yeah. You still are."

The armadillo trotted on in front of him, not saying anything, with his ears pricked against the evening dark.

Eglamarck stood watch that night, while the two humans slept.

The eyesight of armadillos isn't very good, but their hearing is excellent. He could barely see his two companions, rolled up in their blankets in the shadow of a fallen tree, but he could hear their breathing clearly.

Ghuls. A teenage musician with a murderer chasing him. Hmm. While it was certainly safer with another person to keep watch, Oliver and the armadillo might be in more danger travelling with him. The armadillo had not known many murderers in his life, but he had a feeling that once you started killing people for fun, you didn't stop. A boy and an armadillo might not interest the homicidal mayor, but then again, they might. Better to be forewarned.

An owl called off in the distance. The armadillo crouched instinctively. Owls did not generally prey on armadillos, but the oldest parts of the armadillo's brain knew a predator when they heard one.

He wasn't comfortable in the forest. Forests were not armadillo country. He liked deep dirt untroubled by tree roots. Shrubs were okay, and farmland was nice, but trees... he wasn't sure about all these trees.

He listened for the crackle of twigs that might herald a ghul plowing through the forest and heard nothing.

If only Oliver had been older! A better wizard, one at the height of his powers, could have wrapped them up in a spell that made them seem to be logs or ferns. Nothing as showy as invisibility, but just as useful.

He wished he could make Oliver understand that. Big spells

were impressive, sure, but the little ones could be far better for the purpose at hand. Look at all the mileage that Oliver got from the *pushme pullme* spell. But no, Oliver was young enough to feel that he constantly had to prove himself... and to be fair, the people of his village didn't help much.

"Treat you like a small child until they need you, and then expect you to move heaven and earth and bring down rain," the armadillo muttered under his breath. Oliver actually had been very understanding about the whole thing, but he was still irritated on his wizard's behalf.

He raked the leaf litter with his claws.

His display of temper turned up a sleepy grub, and the armadillo pounced on it and swallowed it down.

A spell to turn up grubs—now that would be something! You could keep your invisibility. Stupid spell. Only useful against other humans, really, or maybe birds. You could smell right through it, and unless the wizard stood still and didn't breathe, he'd be obvious to anyone who cared to listen. Leave it to a human wizard to come up with something that fooled the eyes and nothing else.

Well. Still. Oliver was *his* wizard and had been ever since he walked through the door of the old wizard's cottage, a blurry, distant shape with a smell that said *Home.* And *Mine.* Eglamarck couldn't do more than waddle at that point, but he'd struck out determinedly across the ocean of floorboards and up to the enormous blur and marked it as belonging to him.

Now his wizard was in danger, and not the sort you could fix by rolling up in a ball. (Not that he *could* roll into a ball. He was a nine-banded armadillo, and unlike some of his distant cousins, things didn't fit perfectly together. The best he could do was hunch his armored back up and tuck his head under his claws, which was fairly close.) Hmm.

He sniffed the air again.

There was something odd in the forest. *Well, obviously,* he thought, faintly annoyed at himself. His thoughts were getting sloppy as a human's. But there was something just at the edges of his senses. Not magic. Magic had a definite taste and smell. This was something else, an aftertaste to the world, something like leafmould and shadow that lingered in his nose just a fraction longer than it should.

For some reason he thought of Trebastion's song, of the murdered woman still walking under the trees. *Bah. Getting superstitious, too.* It was the sort of ridiculous thing a human might do, coming back as a ghost instead of getting on with the business of being reborn, like any sensible being. Still, the armadillo had his doubts. Humans loved to blame ghosts for things, his mother had said, but she'd never seen one.

Still, between the ghuls and the strange aftertaste, he wanted to get through Harkhound as quickly as possible.

Animals are not broadly troubled by guilt. Eglamarck considered, dispassionately, whether it would be better to abandon Trebastion. The human was not very good in the woods and would probably bring the ghuls down on himself if left alone. Would newly fed ghuls follow after them?

He didn't know. His mother had never mentioned it, if she even knew. He couldn't take the chance that a meal of human flesh would energize their pursuers.

Anyway, Oliver would probably object to abandoning Trebastion. The armadillo had been pleased to see that the company of another human had cheered him up, even if he insisted on spending the last bit of daylight reading up on the invisibility spell.

Well, that was the thing with humans. They liked to be around each other and cram themselves three or four in a den if they could, then cram their dens in together as close as house martin nests. Leave a human alone for too long and it would get weird and sad.

The old wizard had been getting that way, his mother said, until Oliver came along. They'd eased the old man's final years. That was something.

If he didn't want that to be Oliver's only contribution to the world, though, Eglamarck was going to have to come up with a plan to get them to the Rainblades in one piece.

❧

*When you looked at it logically,* Oliver thought, *they had really done quite well.* It took two entire days in the forest before they were hopelessly lost.

"We've gone in a circle," announced the armadillo, about mid-afternoon. "I don't know how we did it, but apparently we did."

"How can you tell?" asked Trebastion. "All these cursed trees look alike. And the shrubs. I had never realized how inter-changeable shrubs are."

"Well, for one thing, I can smell that we passed this way before," said the armadillo. "For the other, that's last night's fire."

Oliver and Trebastion looked dutifully down at the remains of the fire.

"Ah. Hmm," said Trebastion.

Oliver sighed. His pants were already growing loose. Another few meals of cattails, and they'd fall right off.

You couldn't blame the armadillo, though. The forest canopy was so thick that daylight itself was spotty, and there was no way to see the mountains any more. If Oliver had a hard time of it, how much worse would it be if your head was only three inches off the ground?

"High ground," he said. "We need to get to high ground and see if we can't get a good view. A big rock, say, or a hill."

"We could climb a tree," said Trebastion.

They looked up the enormous length of the pines, most of which were three feet across and didn't branch until forty feet up.

"You first," said Oliver.

"Point taken."

"Uphill," said the armadillo. "It's not worth much, but we'll keep going uphill and see if that comes out anywhere."

It is not always easy to determine "uphill" in a forest. The ground undulates gently. Tree roots uplift everything around them. Sudden rainstorms wash away loose earth and create gullies. Oliver put the armadillo over his shoulder and tried to pick a course that went up more often than it went down.

In the end, they came to a steep patch of hillside where a tree had fallen down. There was enough of a gap in the canopy that, by standing on the broken stump, Trebastion could just see over the nearby trees.

"Not much," he reported, turning in a circle. "Trees, trees— hello, what's that?"

"What's what?" Oliver was trying to steady the taller boy's legs.

"Some kind of hill sticking up. No trees on it. And there's ruins, like an old castle or something." He shaded his eyes with his hand. "Well... it'd be a really old castle. A tower, maybe."

"Makes sense," said the armadillo. "You build a watchtower on the highest land you can find, so you can see your enemies coming."

"Let's make for that, then," said Oliver.

It was easier said than done. However easy it is to spot a hill with a ruined keep when you are peering *over* the trees, when you're down *in* them, it's a little more difficult. They had to stop and find an opening in the canopy twice more before they got close enough to make out the rise in the land.

It was getting dark by the time they reached the base of the hill.

"We can sleep in a shelter tonight!" said Trebastion excitedly. "Even if it is just ruins!"

"Walls!" said Oliver happily.

"Race you to the top!"

"Ha!" Oliver took off after Trebastion.

"Now wait a minute..." said the armadillo.

They charged up the grassy hillside and broke from the tree-line.

"Wait!" said the armadillo. "Look, if we've seen the ruins, someone else might have—"

"As long as they've got food!" said Trebastion.

The armadillo scurried along after them as quickly as his little legs would carry him.

And stopped.

And sighed.

Someone else had seen the ruins. Apparently, someone else had seen the ruins quite some time ago.

The bandit camp at the top of the hill had a settled look. The firepit had been dug into the ground. There were hide drapes softening the edges of the ruined tower. And there were a dozen men, all of them with swords and daggers and crossbows.

Swords and daggers and crossbows that were currently pointing at Oliver and Trebastion.

"Well," said the largest bandit, who had one eye and three gold teeth. "Well, well, well. What do we have here?"

Eglamarck melted silently into the undergrowth as the bandits moved toward the humans.

Oliver would have kicked himself, but it wouldn't have helped very much. Also, he might have hit Trebastion by mistake, since they were wedged together in a space barely larger than a closet.

The bandits hadn't been particularly cruel. They had taken Oliver's pack with his spellbooks and his knife, and they had shoved both boys into a small, stuffy enclosure in the back of the ruins, but they hadn't beaten them or hit them or anything like that.

Still, they were quite thoroughly trapped. Stone walls stood on two sides, and the other two had hide drapes over them.

There was not much point in moving the drapes. There was a guard standing right there, and most of the bandits were sitting by the fire less than twenty feet away. Most of the base of the tower was still intact, although the top was open to the sky. The only way in or out of the tower was through a ten-foot tumbledown gap in the wall.

They had also taken Trebastion's lute, so there was that much to be grateful for.

"I feel like an idiot," said Trebastion.

"You and me both," said Oliver.

"Just ran right up, not even thinking. Why did I do that? It could have been the mayor! We're lucky it's *just* bandits."

"Mmm," said Oliver. He wasn't sure how lucky that was. Sure, the bandits hadn't killed them outright, which was good—which was *great!*—but what next? Would they try to ransom them?

The armadillo had gotten away. Oliver wasn't particularly religious, but he thanked whatever gods watched out for wizards that his familiar had avoided capture.

He wondered what the armadillo was doing. Watching, probably. The armadillo would never just abandon him. Familiars and wizards didn't leave each other. If bandits had captured the armadillo, Oliver would have... would have...

Well, he'd have figured something out.

He leaned his back against the stone wall and tried to get comfortable.

Ransom. Hmm. That would be interesting. The villagers from Loosestrife would certainly try to ransom him—and his mother might be back soon, she'd see to it—but what if the bandits didn't want to go all that way? It was days and days, and they didn't have horses.

Would anyone give money for Trebastion?

Maybe the killer who's after him...

That was an unpleasant thought.

"Just ran right into their swords," said Trebastion again. He kicked at the stone wall.

Oliver actually had a pretty good idea why they'd done it. He'd been wandering around so long with a vague distant goal —*Get to the Rainblades, get the rain, get away from the ghuls*—that actually having an immediate goal and reaching it—*The base of the hillside! Right there!*—had gone to his head. He'd been so happy to reach the ruins, even though there was no real point to it, except to maybe see over the trees.

Well, he'd gotten an excellent view over the trees. Unfortunately, he hadn't been paying much attention, because the view over the swords had been so much more immediate.

The leather drape swung aside. "Come on, you two," said the guard. "Out on your feet. The boss wants a look at you."

"Maybe he's looking for a court musician," said Trebastion hopefully.

"He'll probably need to look harder, then," said Oliver.

Trebastion rolled his eyes and climbed out of the tent.

Evening had fallen. The bandits were lit by firelight. Oliver half-expected them to look wild and savage and villainous, but they mostly just looked tired and a bit irritable.

He had expected to be shoved in front of the huge one-eyed man with the gold teeth, but instead the guard steered them to a short, balding man in a patchwork jacket.

He wasn't a terribly impressive figure, but Oliver, meeting his eyes, saw a glitter of intelligence in them.

"Well," said the bandit chief, looking them up and down. "Bit young for rangers. And if you're poachers, you're not armed for it."

"Didn't take any bows off'm," volunteered the guard.

"Let me guess." The bandit chief put his chin in his hand. "You're old enough to be runaway apprentices… possibly indentured servants. Am I right?"

"Not exactly," said Oliver. "I'm a wizard."

A roar of laughter went up from the bandits. The bandit chief shook his head slowly, smiling. "Are you now?"

Oliver felt the tips of his ears get hot. "Um. Well. I—I can do a couple of spells. Not very—well. My village sent me. To bring back the rain."

"Did they, now?" The bandit's smile didn't change. "And if we asked them, would they agree, or would they tell me you'd run away from your master?"

Oliver stared at him. "My master's dead. They'd tell you I came to get rain."

"Dead!" said the bandit. "Did you kill him, then? Little thing like you?"

"No! He was old—he—" Oliver trailed off. His voice sounded

high and childish in his ears and the bandit's grin was getting wider and wider.

It turned out that there was a worse fate than being sent off on a suicide mission by a bunch of grown-ups. It was being sent off on a suicide mission by a bunch of grown-ups *and not having other grown-ups believe you.*

*Doesn't matter,* he thought. *They're bandits. They don't count. Nobody cares what they think. Did you think that if you explained nicely, they'd say, "Oops, sorry, our mistake!" and let you go?*

There was another roar of laughter from the bandits. Trebastion had tried to explain what he did. It hadn't gone over any better than Oliver's explanation had.

"Well," said the bandit chief. He held up a hand, and the other bandits fell silent. "You two certainly have imaginations, I'll give you that." He studied Oliver's face. "All right, then. Suppose you were a wizard. What could you do?"

It was on the tip of Oliver's tongue to utter the words of the *pushme pullme* spell.

*No. He's not going to let us go. It would be very stupid to tell him everything I can do.*

Even though part of him burned to show the bandit chief what he could do, Oliver gritted his teeth and muttered, "I mostly work with herbs."

"Oh, *herbs,*" said the bandit, in the dismissive tone used by people who don't know anything about herbs.

(This is generally not a very wise thing to say, because people who *do* know about herbs may take offense, and you will then find your socks stuffed full of stinging nettles and your tea full of cascara, which is no less potent a laxative for being tree bark.)

Oliver would have given a lot for some cascara bark, and maybe a few minutes alone with the stew bubbling over the fire.

"He's a good wizard!" said Trebastion, who was a little slower on the uptake. "He's got a familiar and everything!"

"It's not much of a familiar," said Oliver, wishing he could stomp on Trebastion's foot. "It's really more like a pet. And it's not like it talks or anything." He hoped the armadillo wasn't listening. "Anyway, it's probably run off now."

"But—"

Oliver gave him a hard look.

Trebastion got the hint and muttered "Well, I don't have a familiar, anyway..." toward the ground.

"This is better than a play," said the bandit chief. "Dear me! I suppose you were both apprenticed to the same wizard?"

"Oh no," said Trebastion. "No. I'm not one at all. Except for the harp thing."

"Out of bones, yes. Strung with hair. Do you know, I never really appreciated the tensile strength of hair before?"

Trebastion turned bright red.

"Ah, well," said the bandit chief. He passed a hand over his own bald skull. "When I'm murdered, you'll have to string the harp with something else, I imagine. Or make a drum."

"Gut might work," said Oliver. "Better sound."

"Oh, indeed." The bandit was clearly enjoying himself immensely. "Well! I have no real use for a wizard, and when we encounter dead people, there is generally no question at all as to how they *became* dead, if you follow me."

The bandit with the gold teeth thumbed the edge of his sword in a meaningful fashion.

"We follow," said Oliver, when Trebastion didn't say anything.

"However, I also don't have much stomach for killing children, so we'll see if we can't make some use of you. I think your village might be quite interested in having you back, runaway or not. Where did you say you were from?"

"Loosestrife," mumbled Oliver. There were only five bandits, near as he could count, and that probably wasn't enough to do much damage to a town of nearly a hundred. Particularly if his mother had gotten back from Wishinghall.

Come to think of it, if the bandits sent for ransom and his mother was back, she'd come and break heads and they could go to the Rainblades with a military escort who happened to be his mom.

"As for you..." The bandit chief turned to Trebastion. "Hmm. Haven't decided what to do about you."

"Slit 'is throat and feed 'em to the crows," growled the gold-toothed bandit.

The bandit chief shook his head sadly. "You have all the empathy of a roasted lizard-on-a-stick, Bill, with a far less pleasant aroma. Besides, if you kill someone now, you don't have the opportunity to make a profit on them later. If nothing else, he can wash the dishes."

Bill muttered something and thumbed his sword-edge again.

Oliver sighed.

In the end, he and Trebastion were given the scraping from the bottom of the stew pot. They did the dishes, and then they were sent back to the little hide tent, to sleep on a couple of grain sacks.

"Wouldn't you know it?" said Oliver. "The best meal and the best bed I've had in a week, and it's after we've been captured by bandits."

"I don't suppose your master had any sage wisdom for this situation?" asked Trebastion hopefully. "Something wizardly and... err... useful?"

"Huh?" Oliver thought about it. As the wizard had gone increasingly senile, it got hard to separate sage wisdom from dementia. "Well... he used to say that if your fly is open, you're better off buttoning it up than spending ten minutes arguing you meant to leave it open."

Trebastion considered this.

"Very wise," he said.

"Oh very."

"Not so helpful to our current situation, though."

"We mostly talked about herbs."

Trebastion snorted loudly. "I just hope Mayor Stern doesn't turn up," he whispered. "He probably *would* pay money for me."

"I kind of hope the ghuls show up," Oliver whispered back. "I bet that Bill guy would make short work of them."

He pulled the drape aside a crack and peered out. The fire had died down, but there was a sentry at the entry of the tower. From the other hide tents came the sounds of snoring.

The sentry looked depressingly alert. Even if he hadn't, there was a bedroll by the fire. Steel gleamed redly in the darkness.

Bill of the gold teeth slept with his sword next to his pillow.

*Even if we could sneak past Bill and do something to the sentry, we'd be in the woods. I might get away, but Trebastion's like a wounded ox. They'd find us in no time.*

A thought formed down in the very bottom of his mind, just a glimmer, no bigger than a tadpole at the bottom of a well.

*I could leave him—*

*No.*

He rolled over, uncomfortable to have even thought such a thing.

Leaving Trebastion behind would be wrong. As wrong as sending a twelve-year-old boy out to die, on the chance of bringing back rain.

I'm better than Harold. I have to be better than that.

His last thought, as he fell down into sleep, was, *I hope the armadillo's okay.*

The armadillo was fine, insofar as a familiar separated from his wizard is ever fine. He had found a couple of slugs. They were not nearly as good as the slugs in the vegetable garden back home, but they were filling, he'd give them that.

He had paced a circuit of the hillside, which was a much more serious matter for an armadillo than a human.

Oliver and Trebastion were inside the ruined tower. He didn't dare get too close to the bandits, though. There's a certain sort of person for whom every moving thing is target practice.

The armadillo waited until darkness fell. When the woods were deep and dark and creaking in the night, he climbed the hill.

The sentry was staring into the darkness, for all the good it did him. Whistles and grunts and all-purpose snores came from inside the tower.

Eglamarck crept through the grass to the edge of the circle of firelight.

The sentry stared off over the familiar's head.

For humans, darkness is a problem. For armadillos, it's a natural state.

When he was confident that most of the bandits were sleeping, the armadillo backed away from the firelight and trotted around the back of the tower.

At a certain point, he stopped.

Wizards have more senses than ordinary people do. They can detect magic in other wizards, feel the presence of demons, and a few—the very powerful ones—can taste time passing, which tends to make them cranky.

Familiars have all those senses and one more—the ability to know, without question, where their wizard is at all times.

Eglamarck knew, beyond a shadow of a doubt, that Oliver was on the other side of this particular stone.

He examined the stone without much hope. It looked to weigh at least a ton.

Five minutes of digging was enough to confirm that the floor of the tower was also stone, and there would be no burrowing to the rescue.

That left him with only one alternative.

Eglamarck sighed, curled up into as tight a ball as he could, and sent his mind into the darkness.

*Hey.*

*Hey.*

*Oliver.*

*You. Yes. Hey. Pay attention!*

Oliver opened one eye in the darkness.

Somebody was talking inside his head. It sounded like—

"Armadillo?"

*Not out loud, unless you want to wake the guards. Also, it makes you sound crazy.*

"But I don't know how to think at you," he whispered.

The voice sighed in his head. *Just pretend you're talking, only don't move your lips. Like learning to read silently instead of out loud.*

Oliver struggled with this concept for a minute, then—

LIKE THIS?

*Can you think any quieter? It's like a gong in there.*

SORRY. IS THIS BETTER?

*Not... really. Never mind. Not important.*

HOW ARE YOU DOING THIS?

*I'm a familiar. You're my wizard. It's a thing we can do.*

YOU NEVER DID IT BEFORE!

*Never really saw the point. Anyway, I wasn't sure if I could until I tried, and there was a small chance you'd go mad, so I didn't want to risk it.*

GO—WAIT. HOW *SMALL A CHANCE?* Oliver opened both eyes and stared up in the darkness.

*Vanishingly minor, I should think. Although if you start hearing a bunch of other voices in here, and I'm just one of them, then we may have a problem.*

The armadillo was the only voice that Oliver could hear. It felt like thinking, only he wasn't sure what he was going to think next.

WAIT. HOW DO I KNOW I'M NOT JUST MAKING THIS ALL UP IN MY HEAD ANYWAY?

The mental sigh seemed to rattle the inside of his skull. *You don't. And no, I can't prove it to you.*

YOU COULD TELL ME SOMETHING I WOULDN'T KNOW—

*And you wouldn't know if you were telling yourself the truth or not, so what good is that?*

Defeated (and baffled) by this logic, Oliver closed his eyes again.

*Let's pretend you're not insane and not dreaming and I'm really talking to you, and when I see you again, I promise to give you a nip on the shin to prove it's all happening.*

ALL RIGHT. CAN YOU GET US OUT OF HERE?

*Oh, sure. My single-pawed assault upon the bandit nest will be the stuff of legend. Mothers will whisper my name to their kits for years to come.*

YOU DON'T HAVE TO BE SARCASTIC ABOUT IT.

*Sorry.*

IT FEELS VERY POINTY IN HERE WHERE YOU'RE SARCASTIC.

*Yes, well. It would be awfully pointy out here when the bandits saw me.*

Oliver thought hard. He was starting to feel the edges of the armadillo in his mind, an odd sort of shadow on the back of his eyes.

DO YOU THINK...

*Hmm?*

*CAN YOU GET TO MY PACK? WITH MY SPELLBOOK?*

Oliver squeezed the bridge of his nose with his fingers. If he could get to the spellbook, maybe he could use the invisibility spell, and they could just walk out of here—

*Won't work. First off, I doubt you can even do the spell on yourself, let alone Trebastion, and second, they'd still notice all the tent flaps moving about. And I probably can't get to the spellbook anyway, unless they leave it lying around outside the tower.*

Oliver stifled a sigh.

CAN YOU GO FOR HELP? MAYBE TO MOM?

There was a long silence in his head. Then: *I don't want to leave you here. Something might happen to you. You might need me. And* —he had a feeling of the shadow shifting its weight awkwardly— *if something happened to you, I'd just be a normal armadillo again. I couldn't even tell your mother where to find you.*

Oliver felt touched and a little sad, all at the same time.

He'd never really thought about it. When the old wizard had died, his familiar had died the same night, curled up at his feet, and they'd buried them together.

OKAY. WELL, IN THAT CASE... I THINK I'M GOING TO NEED SOME HERBS.

༺✿༻

It was a long, tedious morning in the bandit's camp.

They were set to dig a new latrine trench. A bandit sat a few feet away, carrying a crossbow, which put to flight any thoughts of either fleeing or a clandestine meeting with the armadillo.

It was hot, heavy work. The ground was made up of rocks and tree roots. Using the shovel was less a matter of digging and more of wedging the point into a crack and levering the handle back and forth until something popped loose.

Around noon, life got exciting. Oliver wished that it hadn't.

Bill of the gold teeth came down the hillside and said "You. Bring 'em," to the bandit.

"I've got a name, you know," said the bandit.

Bill spat and walked away.

"He seems pleasant," said Trebastion.

"He's an ass," said the bandit. "First he's rude to you and then he gets drunk and breaks your arm. This isn't the life I signed up for, let me tell you."

"We didn't sign up for this either," said Oliver.

"No one ever does," said the bandit philosophically. He gestured with the crossbow, and the two boys headed up the hillside.

They were halfway up the hill when Trebastion froze.

"Oh no..." he whispered.

Oliver looked up to the ruined tower. The bandit chief was standing out front, talking to a stranger.

The newcomer was about six feet tall, with a heavy paunch

and thinning hair. His face was red, and he was gesticulating wildly.

"It's Mayor Stern," said Trebastion.

"Your mayor, I take it?"

"He's not *my* mayor. My mayor was a little old lady from my home village, wouldn't hurt a fly. This guy kills little girls and buries them in the wheat fields."

The friendly bandit gave them a friendly shove. They started moving again.

The bandit chief had a faint smile on his face. Bill stood behind him, thumbing the edge of his sword. Oliver wondered vaguely how he hadn't sliced his thumb to ribbons by now.

There were a half-dozen men farther down the hillside, clutched together like chicks. Like the bandits, they had weaponry, although no crossbows. Unlike the bandits, they looked distinctly ill at ease.

"Other people from the town," whispered Trebastion. "They're mostly relatives, I think."

Some of the men did have a family resemblance to Mayor Stern. Others, though, had a look that Oliver had seen before, in the faces of the crowd that had driven him out town.

It was a look that said, We don't really like this, but we've gone too far to stop. It said, It's easier to keep going than to turn around.

"There!" shouted Mayor Stern, pointing at Trebastion. "That's him! That's the murderer!"

"I am not!" Trebastion shouted back. "You're the one that killed those kids! I just made the harp!"

"Fascinating," said the bandit chief, almost to himself.

Oliver watched one of the men behind the Mayor. His face had gone completely blank when Trebastion spoke, as if whatever he was thinking was not allowed to come out where it could be seen.

It's not just facing that the Mayor's a murderer, thought

Oliver. It's facing that he's been going along with a murderer. It'd be so much easier for him if it was Trebastion...

"You see?" said the Mayor, turning back to the chief. "You must give him to me for justice!"

Trebastion turned pale. Oliver grabbed his arm. The older boy looked ready to bolt, and if he did that, he was going to wind up with a crossbow bolt between his shoulder blades.

"*Must* I?" said the bandit chief slowly. "I'm afraid I don't see that at all."

"Justice must be served!" shouted the Mayor.

"I certainly hope not," said the bandit chief. "I've been avoiding justice for a number of years now. It seems to have worked so far."

The Mayor was turning redder by the minute, and Trebastion was turning greener. Oliver tightened his grip on Trebastion's arm.

The friendly bandit nudged them closer to the campsite. For once, Oliver was glad that Bill was there. The gold-toothed thug stood behind the bandit chief and looked as if he would be happy to stab anybody who moved.

Mayor Stern leveled a shaking finger. "Surely you must see that this cannot be allowed to go unpunished!"

"But I don't see that at all," said the bandit chief. "What I see is that your men are trying to slink away down the hillside and that my men have all the crossbows."

Several men who had been in the Mayor's party immediately stopped inching for the treeline and tried to look as if they hadn't been going anywhere.

The Mayor took a deep breath.

And then, quite suddenly, his manner changed. It was as if the yelling had all been an act, and when he realized that it wasn't getting him anywhere, he moved smoothly onto the next thing. "Very well. You seem to be a reasonable man. I'm sure that we can come to a mutually beneficial arrangement."

"That's better," said the bandit chief. "Bill, see our two—

guests—inside, just in case Mister Stern gets any ideas." He smiled pleasantly.

Mayor Stern looked over at Oliver and Trebastion. His eyes passed over Oliver, and the minor mage felt a shudder crawl up his spine, as if a cockroach had just scuttled over his feet.

*There's something all twisted up inside him. It's like he's another ghul, but only on the inside.*

Oliver felt as if he'd picked up a piece of rotting meat and felt things squirming under his fingers.

He looked away, to the bandit chief, and saw something fixed and sharp about the man's smile.

*He sees it, too. He doesn't trust him either.*

"Inside," said the chief to Oliver and Trebastion. "Can't risk anything happening to the little lambs, can we?"

"Of course not," said Mayor Stern, with his fake, squirming smile.

"At least," said the bandit chief, as Trebastion and Oliver plodded into the tower, "not while we're discussing the price of mutton..."

## ❧ 8 ❧

"We have to get out of here!" hissed Trebastion. "We have to get out of here right now!"

"The guards are still there," said Oliver. "Bill hasn't gotten any smaller. I don't think we're going anywhere."

He did have a plan—or part of one—if the armadillo could find the right herbs, but it was going to require at least one meal to work. You could do a lot with herbs, but you had to get them inside people first. Just waving leaves at their captors wasn't going to do much.

Trebastion was in no mood to listen to reason. "If Stern gets me—Do you *know* what he did to those kids?"

"Actually, no," said Oliver. "And I don't really want to, either." Someone with a smile like that would be capable of things that Oliver couldn't even begin to imagine.

"The harps were *relieved* to be dead," said Trebastion. "They hated me for bringing them back and making them remember what had happened. Almost as much as they hated *him*. Oh lord, I wonder what they did with the harps?"

"I'm less worried about the harps than about us." Oliver peered out of the tent flap. What he saw was the back of Bill's calves. He let the tent flap close again.

"He won't want you," said Trebastion miserably. "Unless he thinks I've told you things, and he probably won't care. But he'll take me back, even if he has to kill every bandit to do it."

"He can't do that," said Oliver.

"He'd do it in a heartbeat! He's a monster!"

"No, no," said Oliver, patting Trebastion's shoulder, "I mean he *can't*. He hasn't got the men, and the men he's got are all farmers. I wouldn't mess with them at hog butchering time, but I was looking, and they don't have axes or even pitchforks. The chief's got crossbows. And Bill."

Trebastion exhaled slowly. "You're right. Right. Okay."

They sat in silence for a moment. Oliver could hear Stern's voice raised, but couldn't make out the words.

"He might sell me, though," said Trebastion glumly. "To Stern."

"He might," said Oliver. Privately he thought this was likely. The bandit chief had not liked Stern, but he didn't have to like him to take his money. And people who lived in the woods and preyed on travelers tended not to have hearts of gold, no matter what the cheery legends said.

"If he does, I'm dead meat."

Oliver put his chin in his hand.

"Maybe," he said finally. "But think about it. Do you think his men know what he's really like? You said they were mostly relatives, and that he'd whipped them into a lynch mob."

If Harold the miller back home had been killing people and stuffing them under the floorboards of the mill... Well, Oliver would have found them, frankly, he'd been all over the mill during that imp infestation.

And murder victims tend to do weird magical things to the ground. I'd have noticed. There's that one patch out by Vezzo's farm where there was a gibbet a hundred years ago, and you still can't plant potatoes within fifty feet of it.

You really only have to see a potato bleed once before you become very careful with the plantings.

Still. Supposing that Harold had *been* murdering people. None of the townspeople would want to believe it. They wouldn't want someone they knew to be a murderer. Harold would yell about his innocence, and people would agree...

...up to a point.

But if Harold went over the line and somebody caught him— if he even did something overly *suspicious*—the other townspeople would turn on him. Being a pillar of the community wouldn't protect him.

In fact, they'd be much, much angrier than if they'd believed he was a murderer in the first place, because they'd be mad at themselves for not stopping him sooner.

"I *think*," said Oliver slowly, "they're scared. They're sort of a mob, you understand? They're following Stern because he's yelling the loudest, the way that the people in my town followed Harold the miller when he started yelling that I needed to go bring back rain." He leaned back, closing his eyes. Two crowds, two sets of frightened, angry faces... "Thing is, this has gone too far. Most of them don't quite know what's going on any more, and they don't like it. If Stern goes too far, they'll realize that he really is a monster. But if they accept *that,* they have to accept that they were wrong in the first place, and that they've been helping a monster all along."

"Okay," said Trebastion. "So, what do you think that means?"

"I think if he convinces the chief to sell you, you'll be okay at first," said Oliver. "He might rough you up a little, but he's not going to do anything really awful to you while the others are around. It's when he gets you back to town that you need to worry."

"I'm just going to start worrying *now*, if it's all the same to you," said Trebastion. "It's all very well to say that he's only going to rough me up a *little,* but it's still going to hurt. And what if you're wrong, and they're a whole hunting pack of deviants?"

"Then you're in trouble," said Oliver.

In the silence that followed, they could both hear Stern yell, very clearly, "Are you out of your mind? I could buy fifty acres of land for that!"

"Well," said Oliver, "at least you're costing him a lot of money."

"You'll forgive me if that's not much consolation."

Several hours passed, and the sun was starting to crawl down the sky before the tent flap opened and Bill reached in and pulled Trebastion out.

"Time to go, minstrel-boy," said Bill, licking his gold teeth.

Trebastion's face went the color of old cheese.

Bill dragged him across the tower. Trebastion struggled, but not very hard (there was a limit to how much you could struggle against someone the size of Bill).

Oliver hurried after them. Nobody yelled "stop!" so presumably nobody was watching. He halted in the shadow of one of the tents and peered around the edge.

"This is highway robbery," Stern was grumbling, counting out gold pieces into the bandit chief's hand.

"Robbery, certainly," said the bandit chief pleasantly. "But what did you expect from a bandit?"

"By rights I ought to have you hauled in and slapped in the stocks," growled Stern.

"Careful, now," said the chief. "Don't talk yourself out of a deal—that coin's been clipped, friend, let's see you replace it with a better one—when you're so close."

There was an unaccustomed edge to the bandit's voice. Oliver leaned farther out of the shadow and studied the man closely.

*He doesn't like this. He knows that Stern's going to do something pretty awful to Trebastion when he gets a chance.*

*He's still going to take the money, though.*

"There," said Stern. "Is that all to your liking?"

"As much to my liking as it shall get," said the chief lightly. He hefted the coins in his hand several times.

"Then give me the boy," said Stern.

"As you wish. Bill—"

Bill picked Trebastion up by the scruff of the neck and carried him toward Stern's men. They all fell back a step. Oliver moved to the edge of the tower, trying to see his friend's face.

No, no, this is really happening, they've really got him, I should do something—!

"Don't do this!" screamed Trebastion. "He's going to kill me like he did those kids—please, don't let him get me—"

Bill dropped him. Trebastion scrambled to his feet and made a break through the back of the crowd. One of Stern's men grabbed for him. Stern himself lunged into the fray and nearly ran into Bill, who growled and put a hand on the hilt of his sword.

Several of the bandits took a step forward. Someone cocked a crossbow.

Oliver would have stood at the tower entrance, watching, until the whole mess had sorted itself out, but a voice yelled in his head, *Now, you idiot, go NOW while no one is looking!*

The armadillo. Of course.

Oliver took a quick look around, saw that all eyes were fastened on the scene, and ducked around the edge of the tower wall. A few quick steps and he was behind the tower. He could hear yelling behind him.

"Hold him, you fool!"

"Do something!"

"If you can't take care of your purchases, it's none of my affair..."

Oliver ran for the trees.


He almost made it. He could actually see the ridges in the bark of the nearest tree, and then a hand closed over his collar and jerked him backward. Oliver hit the ground, the air going out of him in a woosh.

He looked up, and up, and up. The view didn't get any better.

"And where do you think you're going?" asked Bill. "Thought you'd get away while we were looking the other way, did you?"

"I had to pee?" Oliver said weakly. His ribs felt bruised.

There was a thought in his head that had to be an armadillo obscenity. It sounded like a cat hissing and stank like sour beer. It drowned out the real world for a few seconds, but that was probably all right. Bill was not saying anything that Oliver wanted to hear.

"...your *feet* if you try that again," Bill finished.

Oliver could see up Bill's nostrils. This was not a view that he had been curious about.

Bill picked him up by the collar like a kitten, ignoring the choking noises as the fabric cut into Oliver's neck, and carried him back to the camp. "Inside," he said, tossing him toward the tiny enclosure in the back.

Trebastion and Stern were already gone. The friendly bandit shook his head ruefully at Oliver. "Tired of our company already?"

Oliver mumbled something and scurried into the crude tent in the back.

Well. Now what?

*Sit tight, his familiar said. I'll be back soon.*

The armadillo's presence in his head seemed to get more and more attenuated, as if his familiar was going away. Oliver didn't like that at all, but maybe the armadillo was going for help.

He just hoped that help would get there in time.

۞

The armadillo was indeed going for help, but not in the sense that Oliver had been thinking.

Instead, he had found the Bryerlys.

It was late afternoon and the ghuls lay asleep in a hollow in the forest floor. The sickly-sweet smell of illness and ant eggs poured off them.

Vision wasn't the armadillo's keenest sense, but they looked less human than they had at the farm. Perhaps without the trappings of humanity, the chairs and tables to sit in and beds to sleep in, they had slid further away from their roots. The armadillo had always vaguely suspected that humans acted the way they did because they had so much furniture cluttering up their lives.

Or they get more ghul-like when they're hungry. The scaled ancestors only know.

One's long arm was outflung, mouth open against the dirt and leaves. Its nails were long and dirty, and it had torn furrows in the leaf litter in its sleep. The other was curled up, but less like a sleeping animal and more like a dead spider.

He backed away. He wasn't sure if the ghuls would be able to smell him, but he didn't want to risk it.

While he had been trying to find the herbs for Oliver—and mostly failing—he'd come across a scent trail that had filled him with relief.

*Pig.* And not a huge hairy wild boar, the sort that could tear up a man or a hunting hound the way that the armadillo tore up an ant nest, but familiar pigs. The sow and the boar had made their lumbering way to Harkhound.

He'd smelled them on the road once or twice, but apparently they had cut across the fields and taken a more direct route. He'd lost them days before reaching Harkhound Forest, but here they were.

Once he picked up the trail again, he moved with better speed. Pigs could disappear with astonishing skill when they chose, but these two weren't bothering to hide. They were just making their way through the forest, stopping to roll around, scrape up against trees, and dig up anything that looked tasty.

He hoped that wouldn't include armadillo. Pigs had good memories, but they also had endless appetites.

Still, they were the closest he had to friends in these woods right now.

Eglamarck squared his scaled shoulders and trotted deeper into the forest.

⸙

Oliver woke from a deep sleep because someone had screamed.

It was a hoarse male scream of pain and it was bad. But then there was a wet ripping sound and the scream stopped and that was a great deal worse.

*What is going on? Are we under attack?*

His first instinct was to run out and see what the screaming had been and if he could do anything. He got as far as his hand on the blanket flap before he thought, *What if it's the ghuls? Or Stern?* and had a strong urge to retreat back into the corner.

*Don't be stupid. A blanket isn't going to save you. They'll find you.*

Oliver opened the flap an inch and put his eye to it. All he could see was splashes of moonlight and movement. There was something large in the camp. Two somethings.

Bill roared with rage and then he heard a loud squeal, like... a pig?

Something struck the side of the crude hide shelter and nearly knocked it down.

*Run!* shouted the armadillo in his head. *Run quick! Around the back of the tower, while they're distracted!*

Oliver obeyed. He flung himself through the blankets and ran, keeping low. He saw a huge shadow that had to be Bill, but the bandit's back was to him.

*Don't get in front of the pigs. They can't see very well and they're getting worked up.*

The armadillo didn't have to tell him twice. He could see the pigs moving in the firelight, great hairy blurs of hide and rage. There was a shape on the ground that looked human that wasn't moving at all. *The chief? Or someone else?* Bill had his sword out and was slicing at one of the pigs, but either he wasn't connecting or the pig didn't feel it.

*Go, go!* The armadillo sounded frantic. *Hurry!*

Oliver stumbled around the back of the tower, tripping over things, and nearly fell. His own knapsack almost sent him sprawling a second time. Fortunately, the bandits were far more concerned with the pigs than with him. He snatched up the sack and ran.

His heart was hammering as he sprinted down the hillside. A small scaly shadow was waiting for him, just inside the treeline. He darted out, and as promised, nipped Oliver on the shin.

Oliver scooped his familiar up, half-sobbing. The armadillo licked the side of his face and said, "No time, now! Run!"

Then there was only running and shouted directions from the armadillo. They were going somewhere. Oliver didn't care where that was, just as long as it was away from the bandits and the furious pigs.

"Here," panted the armadillo. "In here! Quick!"

Oliver wasn't sure how far he'd come in the woods. Not nearly far enough, probably. He was badly out of breath and at any moment, the ghuls would come for him.

The armadillo was also panting, but he had insisted on running instead of being carried.

His familiar skidded to a halt in front of a tree stump. An enormous shell of bark had calved off, leaving a rotten hollow behind.

"Are—you—sure?" Oliver put his hands on his knees and gasped for air.

"Scouted it last night," the armadillo said. "You can't outrun the bandits, so better to hide."

"But Trebastion—"

"Later. We won't leave him. But you can't help if you're caught. Get in the tree."

Oliver crawled into the tree stump. The rotten bit extended into the ground itself about six inches, so when he was curled into the hole, his head was about knee-level.

Oliver heard a distant shout and cringed. The bandits had to be on his trail now. He didn't know how much woodcraft they had, but surely it was obvious which way he'd gone, even in the fading evening light.

The armadillo flipped at the sheet of bark with his snout. "Come on, you've got thumbs. Pull it into place. Use the spell."

Oliver dragged the bark shell as far up the tree by hand as he could. He gritted his teeth. *Pushme... pullme...*

After the wooden bar in the ghul's barn, it was easy. The bark had a great deal of bulk but hardly any weight. The real problem was getting a grip on it in the first place.

"Higher!" whispered the armadillo. "A few inches higher, and nobody'll be able to tell there's a hole at all. Hurry!"

*Pushme... pushme...*

*If I could go invisible, I wouldn't have to worry about this!*

"Got it!" said the armadillo. Oliver heard scuffling outside. "I'll hide your tracks. Don't make a sound. If you have to communicate, do it mentally."

There were more scuffling noises, going away from the tree.

Oliver hunched his shoulders up to his ears. *I have been spending far too much time lately hiding from people.*

At least there weren't lilac twigs poking him in the ear this time. And the bandits probably wouldn't eat him if they caught him.

On the down side, his lower back was going numb from being curled in such an awkward position, a book was digging into his back, and something small and wiggly with a great many legs was crawling around his ankle.

*Please let it be a millipede. If a centipede bites me, I'm going to yelp because those hurt. Please let it be a millipede.*

He heard a thump and the crunch of leaves as someone approached.

The wiggly thing wandered around his left sock. Oliver closed his eyes and thought, *millipede millipede millipede...*

"Damn little rat," said Bill, practically over his head. "Can't see a damn thing in the dark."

Oliver stopped thinking about invisibility or millipedes and threw all his mental effort into the *pushme pullme* spell. If the bark shell fell off while Bill was standing there...

"Well, there wasn't any money in that one," said another bandit. Oliver thought it might be the friendly one from earlier. "We weren't gonna walk five days through farmland to ransom him. I say we go back. We're not gonna find him in the dark, we still gotta bury Sid, and I think the chief's hurt worse than he let on."

There was a soggy thud as somebody kicked the tree stump. The bark shell tried to slip and Oliver flung his mental arms around it. *Pushme! Pushme! Hold still, hold still!*

"It's why I want him," growled Bill. "What he done to Sid."

"You think it was him? Looked like a boar to me."

"What's a boar doing coming up the hill? Let alone two of 'em? It was wizarding, that's what it was. Those things were his familiars or demons or somethin'."

"If you say so, Bill." The friendly bandit sounded unconvinced. "He's probably a mile away by now, though. Thought I saw some broken branches this way, but I'm not a bloodhound."

"Chief's gonna be mad," growled Bill.

"Chief's got bigger things to worry about. And he got double the ransom for t'other one that he'd been expecting."

Someone—probably Bill—spat on the ground. "Should have gutted that Stern fellow and looted his corpse."

"For once I'm agreeing with you, Big Bill..."

Oliver was concentrating so hard and his teeth were clamped so tightly together that at first he almost didn't understand the sound that followed.

Footsteps.

Going *away*.

A few minutes later, the armadillo nosed the bark aside and climbed into the tree stump. "They're gone," he said. "Did you know you've got a millipede on your shoe?"

Oliver put his arms around his familiar and astonished himself by bursting into tears.

"I'm fine," he sobbed to the astonished armadillo. "I'm fine. I'm okay. It's fine." Since he was still crying, it was nearly impossible to make the words out, but his familiar got the gist.

"You don't sound fine," said the armadillo.

"I'm... fine..." Oliver insisted, bent double with sobs.

His familiar wisely stopped arguing and began licking his face instead.

"Sorry," croaked the mage a few minutes later. "Just... everything. Sorry."

"Surprised you didn't do it before now," said the armadillo matter-of-factly. "Humans need to let stuff out or they get weird. Better now?"

"I think so," said Oliver, sitting up. He took a deep breath, which caught a little at the bottom, and concentrated on letting it out slowly. "Yeah. Better. That was the pigs from the farm, wasn't it?"

The armadillo nodded. "They don't really understand a favor for a favor, but they understand helping. And after the Bryerlys, I think they wanted some revenge on something shaped like a human."

Oliver gulped. *We have to bury Sid.* He didn't know which one had been Sid, but whoever it was, they were dead. And Oliver was the reason.

He couldn't very well blame the pigs for saving his life, but some part of him—the part that grew up with farmers—was screaming that he'd let two hogs loose in the woods and got them to kill humans and that was an act as evil as anything the bandits had done.

But it was done. And he wasn't going to blame the armadillo for it. The armadillo hadn't been the one stupid enough to get captured and need the help.

"I can still hear you thinking, you know," said his familiar wearily.

Oliver put his face in his hands. "I hate this," he said, surprised at how conversational his voice sounded.

"I know." The armadillo leaned against his leg. After a moment, as if unsure whether this would help or not, he added, "Your mother's killed people."

Oliver gave a croaking laugh. "Yeah," he said, scrubbing at his face. "Yeah, she has." He'd never really thought about it before. His mother was... well, she was *good.* She'd been a warrior and even retired, she was fierce and strong and kind. Oliver would have given anything to have her here with him. She could tell him how he was supposed to feel right now, about Sid and Bill and all of it.

But she wasn't here. And Oliver had gotten free, with help from his friends.

"Are the pigs okay?" he asked.

"Don't know," said the armadillo. "We need to check, but I don't want to go stomping around in the woods in the dark with ghuls and bandits wandering around. Wait until moonrise and we'll get away from the tower, and then decide what happens next."

Moonrise took a long time. Oliver actually dozed off, which astonished him when he woke up. (The armadillo was less astonished. Humans, his mother had told him, laugh or cry or rage when they get pushed too far, and then they usually fall asleep. The armadillo's mother had been a clear-eyed observer of humanity, even if her eyes were only a few inches off the ground.)

When Oliver woke, the armadillo was gone. He would have been worried, but his back and neck and left leg were letting him know that sleeping curled in a ball in a tree stump was a really terrible idea, and by the time he had massaged some feeling back into his foot, the armadillo was back.

"I've found the trail," the armadillo said.

"Of the pigs?"

The armadillo rolled his eyes. "That's not a trail. That's practically a road. They're waiting for us. No, I meant the people who took Trebastion. Are we going to follow or try to get away?"

"Follow, of course," said Oliver, surprised that his familiar would even ask. "We've got to get him away from that man!"

The armadillo nodded. "I thought you'd say that," he said. "It's just that the odds are that we'll be horribly murdered by this Mayor Stern fellow, and then no one will be bringing rain anywhere."

"Yes, well." Oliver climbed out of the tree trunk and tried to straighten his back with a hiss of pain. "This trip has been nothing but people wanting to murder us horribly."

"There's that." The armadillo set off through the woods. "Pigs first."

꧁꧂

The armadillo was right. While Oliver had often been astonished by the ability of a pig to simply vanish, the boar and the sow weren't bothering. They had left a trail of broken trees and churned mud behind them. At one point, they actually had to skirt around a makeshift wallow. The pigs were clearly not worried about pursuit.

Well, when you weigh three or four hundred pounds and you're made of muscle and bristle, you probably don't have to worry much.

Oliver had never felt envious of a hog before. It was a strange sensation.

The first glimpse he caught of them was the white patches on the sow's flanks. They stood out brightly in the moonlight.

"Where's the boar?" whispered Oliver, suddenly sick with dread. Had the boar been injured helping him?

"About three feet to your left," said the armadillo.

Oliver let out an undignified squeak. He turned his head and caught the glint of tiny eyes.

The boar huffed.

"He thought that was funny," translated the armadillo. "Pigs have a fairly... rudimentary... sense of humor."

"Did they get hurt?"

"The boar's been cut, but it's all in the shield fat. He'll be fine. The sow stinks of blood, but it's all human."

Oliver winced. Still, he didn't get to complain. They'd risked their lives for him, and his mother would have given him an earful about ingratitude.

"Can you thank them for me?" asked Oliver. "For saving me?"

"Not really." The armadillo considered. "Let me see what I can do, though."

The armadillo trotted up to the sow. She lowered her head. They breathed at each other, while Oliver tried to inch away from the boar without being too obvious about it.

After a few moments, the armadillo nodded and turned away. "Come on, then."

"We're leaving?"

"They're friendly right now. Let's not push it. They're still pigs."

Oliver lifted a hand. He was pretty sure that the pigs didn't understand waving goodbye, but it made him feel better about it.

"What did you tell them?" he asked, as they pushed through the forest, up the backtrail left by the hogs.

"Good pigs. Good human. Good armadillo. All good. All together and good." The armadillo shrugged. "That's as close as I can get to, *Thank you and we're friends.*"

"Better than I could have done," said Oliver. "Thank you."

"Oh, well..." His familiar snorted briskly. "Now, let's find Trebastion and get on with being horribly murdered."

Oliver grinned. It shouldn't have made him feel better, but somehow it did. "Where's the trail?"

"I had to circle around the bandit camp to reach it the first time, but I think we can pick it up farther away so that we don't get you too close to the bandits... what's left of the bandits..."

"Lead the way."

An hour later, the moon had moved in the sky and the armadillo had admitted defeat.

"I've lost them," he said grimly. "Somewhere along the way. I don't know how, they left a trail like an army, but in these woods... all I know is we should have crossed their track by now. Long *before* now." He uttered a small armadillo curse, which sounded like an angry chuff of air.

"Do we have to go back to the bandit camp and try again?" asked Oliver worriedly.

The armadillo scuffled at the ground. "I suppose we don't have much choice. Gah, at this rate it'll be dawn by the time we find them again... then again, with ghuls about, maybe that's a good thing."

Oliver chewed his lower lip. "I could try to feel for mages," he said slowly. "Trebastion's a mage, even if he's not very much of one. If I could pick up his aura somehow..."

The armadillo sat back on his haunches. "It's worth a try," he said. "The armored ancestors know I don't have any better ideas, anyway."

Oliver sat down and wiggled until he was comfortable. He closed his eyes and tried to open his mind up to the forest.

It wasn't magic, exactly. Magic meant you were *doing* something. This was just sitting and existing and looking.

"Look with your skin," the old wizard had told him once or twice. Oliver wasn't sure if what he was doing was what his master had meant, but it was the closest he'd been able to come. He was never really sure if what he was seeing with his skin was really there or all in his head though.

He also wasn't entirely sure it mattered. Magic was basically all in your head until it wasn't.

What his skin saw now was Harkhound Forest. It was huge. It went on and on, far past the limits of what Oliver could hold in his mind. He felt trees and roots and leaf litter and the armadillo in front of him, like a small, cranky star.

*Trebastion*, he thought. *I am looking for Trebastion. He has a little magic and it stands out around him. Just a little.*

Harkhound was vast and silent and uninterested. The movement of a fern as an insect climbed it was of greater concern to Harkhound than the whereabouts of a human.

*Please?* thought Oliver. *Please, can you help me?*

Silence.

Oliver sagged in disappointment and opened his eyes. "It's no use—" he started to say, and then he caught a glimpse of something red out of the corner of his eye.

It made no sense. The woods were dark, illuminated only by patches of moonlight. Anything red would have looked black. But this had been a swift glimpse of bright red, as clear as daylight, that vanished before he could focus on it.

"What is it?" asked the armadillo.

Oliver shook his head and climbed to his feet. "Something red," he said. "Over here."

"Blood?"

"No..." It hadn't been blood red, but the crimson of an apple or a ripe tomato, a cheerful color completely out of place in a dark forest at night.

He walked toward the place where he had seen the color.

There was nothing there. That didn't actually surprise Oliver much. If he had seen a thing that was visually impossible, then probably he hadn't seen it with his eyes.

*Look with your skin.*

He closed his eyes again and tried to look with his skin.

Darkness. Leaves. The trunks of trees, older than the oldest living human, slow and deeply unimpressed. The call of night insects, rising up from the ground like fog.

Behind his eyelids, another flash of red. Someone ducking away behind a tree?

In his mind, he could hear Trebastion singing.

. . .

In the trees, in the trees,
   Her spirit still walks
   In her kirtle of red
   In the trees, in the trees, in the trees...

"Come on," said Oliver to his familiar. "I think someone wants us to follow them."

"To Trebastion, or to our horrible deaths?" asked the armadillo, waddling after him.

Oliver shrugged. "At this point, I don't know if it matters all that much. We don't have any other guides."

The armadillo muttered something but broke into a trot and followed.

## ❦ 9 ❧

It was a strange, halting journey through Harkhound. Oliver lost their guide twice and had to backtrack. Whatever it was seemed to be trying to give them some kind of direction but vanished like a will-o-the-wisp if he looked at it directly.

"This is how people end up trapped in a dryad's tree for eternity," grumbled the armadillo. "Or... hsst!"

Oliver halted. "What?"

"Something up ahead. I hear—There!"

Light flickered between the trees. Oliver dropped into a crouch, even though realistically he knew that the people at the light were hundreds of yards away and couldn't possibly see him.

"I'll go look," said the armadillo. Oliver nodded.

As soon as the familiar was gone, he closed his eyes and whispered, *"Thank you,"* to whatever their guide had been.

He felt something then, a whisper so soft that it might have been a fern dreaming or the heartbeat of a vole underground. When he opened his eyes, the moonlight was dappled with apple red.

Oliver was already on his knees, but he bowed his head, feeling complicated things he didn't know how to deal with. When kindness came from murdered ghosts and lost pigs, and the adults that were supposed to help you were monsters that walked like men... What was he supposed to do? It wasn't right. He wanted the world to be different.

*But I'm only a minor mage and I don't know how to fix any of this...*

The armadillo's return was heralded by soft huffs of breath. "It's them," he said. "Come on. There's a thicket close enough that you can get near and they won't hear you because... Well, they won't hear you."

Oliver puzzled over that statement until he had crawled within earshot of the camp, and then he didn't have to puzzle any longer, because he could hear the crack of flesh on flesh himself.

Mayor Stern stood over Trebastion; hands raised. As Oliver watched, teeth gritted, Stern's hands rose and fell, striking the minstrel over and over, sometimes with a crack, sometimes with the dull smack of bread dough on a table.

Trebastion wasn't trying to fight back at all. He'd curled into as much a ball as he could manage, shoulders up around his ears, trying to protect his face and his hands.

It took a moment before he could tear his eyes away from the scene. It felt almost like a betrayal. He should be bearing witness somehow, not letting all this pain go by unacknowledged.

*No. No, that's not what will help. I need to scout out guards... defenses... figure out how to get him out...*

This was easier said than done. The bandits had been organized. They had a system and a guard rotation and Oliver had been able to figure out when someone would be looking in any given direction.

Stern's men milled about like a disorganized group of townsmen who didn't have any orders to be anywhere in particular. They'd put out bedrolls, in no discernible pattern. A few were watching Stern and Trebastion, but most of them seemed to be trying very hard not to watch. Their expressions reminded Oliver again of the villager mob, the growing realization that everything had gone too far, and the equally growing despair that there was no way to stop it.

Crack!

Trebastion's drawn out groan fell into a silence in the camp. Several men winced. Two began to talk very loudly to each other about dinner.

"Should kill you right now," Stern said, his breathing thick and heavy. "Not even worth dragging you back home."

"Boss," said one of the men, laying a hand on his arm. "It's not worth it. You want to give that lad a trial, make sure it's all done right and proper."

"He dragged my name through the mud," snapped Stern.

"That he did," said the man, nodding. "And he'll pay for that in court. But you can't go killing him now. Wouldn't look right."

"Feh." Stern shook his arm off. "*Look right.* I know what I know." But the man's words seemed to have calmed him. He cuffed Trebastion one last time, almost perfunctorily, then stalked away to his own bedroll.

🙰

Oliver watched the camp for nearly an hour. He couldn't tell if they were going to set watches or if they were just going to go to sleep. He wasn't even sure if it mattered. He was probably just as likely to wander into someone looking for a place to piss as he was to wander into a sentry.

Trebastion was on the opposite side of the fire. Oliver wondered if he'd be able to run. It didn't look promising. He lay there like a dead thing, and if Oliver hadn't watched closely, he wouldn't have been able to spot the rise and fall of the minstrel's rib cage.

Unfortunately, Stern was between Trebastion and the forest, and showed no signs of moving. He might have been asleep, but Oliver could see an occasional glint of firelight on open eyes. If he was sleeping, it was not deeply or well.

*I hope it's his conscience, but I doubt it.*

Eventually he gave up watching and crept away, timing it when one of the men got up so that his sounds were covered. Stern's men were as loud as Trebastion in the woods. He slipped between tree trunks until he could stand and moved off out of earshot, waiting for the armadillo to find him.

His familiar turned up a few minutes later, mouth still full of slugs. "Wmmpf?" he said and swallowed.

"Not good."

The armadillo grunted. Oliver leaned against a tree and tried to think of something... anything... that might help. "If I could turn invisible, I could walk in..." he began.

"And then what?" said the armadillo. "Say, 'Sorry, don't mind the invisible person carrying your prisoner away?'"

Oliver scowled. He couldn't think of a reply to that.

"Anyway, it doesn't matter. You can't turn invisible. Probably you'll never be able to turn invisible, but you definitely won't be able to in the next hour."

Oliver glared at the armadillo in the dark. "I wish you'd stop that."

"Stop what? I'm your familiar, it's my job to know how much magic you can do."

"So what? You think I should just stop trying to be better, then?" Oliver felt as if something were cracking open in his chest, something raw and red. Watching Stern hit poor Trebastion had left him feeling helpless and furious and now the armadillo was talking down to him and all that fury was piling up and looking for a chance to get out. "Is that your solution? Just be happy with what I can do and never try to do any better? Be content to spend the rest of my life as a minor mage?"

His voice rose as he talked, and he realized it and clamped down so that the last words came out in a harsh squeak.

The armadillo simply looked at him. Black pebble eyes caught a gleam of stray light from the stars. "How many beatings does Trebastion have to take for your personal growth?" he asked quietly.

Oliver felt heat rush to his cheeks. His heart pounded in his ears so loudly that for a moment he did not realize that it wasn't just his heart, it was...

Footsteps.

The armadillo jumped up and leapt into the ferns. "Bandits!"

Oliver caught a flash through the trees.

Starlight.

Off a knife.

*It's Bill, oh god, it's Bill, he's going to see me, I can't possibly run the only reason he hasn't seen me is because I haven't moved but he's going to walk into this clearing and I'll be sitting right here but if I run he'll hear me—*

"Come on!" hissed the armadillo. "Move, move, *move!*"

And then Oliver had an idea.

His spellbook was gone, but he had gone over the invisibility spell a hundred times. He could have recited it in his sleep.

He closed his eyes.

"Oh no—!" said the armadillo. "Damnit, Oliver—"

He tuned out his familiar, his surroundings, his fear. Bill was walking into the clearing, had probably already seen him, but that didn't matter either.

Concentrate. Concentrate. It hasn't worked before, but it didn't need to. It matters now. Just like the bar in the ghul's barn. You can do magic when it counts.

He said the words of the spell.

He could *feel* the power around him, rising up out of the ground like mist. He could feel it wash over his skin, cool against his cheekbones and the backs of his hands.

"Arista... pashtuk... n'gaah..."

There were running footsteps and bellowing and the armadillo moaning, but none of that mattered. The only thing that mattered was the power.

Oliver spoke the last word. The power crackled through him

and was gone. He felt scorched and purified. The air smelled of ozone.

*This must be what it feels like to be a real wizard...*

He opened his eyes.

Bill was running towards him, his knife upraised. Oliver smiled. He was invisible. He had only to step aside and Bill would run right past him.

He stepped to one side and... Bill locked eyes with him.

*Why can he see me?*

The only reason that he didn't die at that moment was because the armadillo shot out of the bushes and in between Bill's feet. The bandit went down with a roar. The armadillo yelped, rolled into a ball, and bounced several feet before coming to his feet.

"...I'm not invisible?" said Oliver.

"You're going to be *dead* in a minute!" screamed the armadillo. "Now *run!*"

Oliver ran.

It took Bill a few minutes to get after him. Oliver could hear him limping through the trees. Apparently, he'd landed badly, or he was still hurt from the pig's attack. He was still terrifyingly quick, though.

"Gonna get you, rat!" he yelled, plowing through the undergrowth. "Gonna get you for what you did to the chief!"

Even in full flight, Oliver found himself thinking *What? I didn't do anything to the chief! I didn't even drug their food! It was all the hogs, not me!*

Bill did not seem interested in the finer points of logical debate.

The armadillo had vanished. He couldn't keep up with the pace. Oliver knew he'd catch up again, but in the meantime he had no idea where he was going and it was only a matter of time before he put his foot in a gopher hole in the dark, and *why* hadn't the spell worked?

*I'm an idiot.*

He gritted his teeth. The armadillo had just *told* him he couldn't do the invisibility spell.

*I didn't want to admit that I was that bad at magic.*

Except... the armadillo had never told him he was bad at magic. His familiar had just told him to do the things he *was* good at.

*I'm definitely an idiot.*

*And I'm still being an idiot. I don't deserve to call myself a wizard.*

There was a tree ahead with an invitingly climbable trunk. Oliver didn't even stop his run. He got a foot on the trunk and went up it to the second set of branches.

Bill was a dozen steps behind him. He reached the base of the tree and grabbed for a low branch. His gold tooth glinted.

"Got you now!"

"Sure," said Oliver.

Bill lifted a foot to put on the trunk and found that his boot-laces were tied together.

He stared at his feet in absolute bafflement, then let out a roar. Oliver took advantage of the delay to climb up to the next branch.

*I go high enough, and the branches won't take his weight. Of course, that might not stop him...*

Bill chopped through his shoelaces with his knife, put his knife between his teeth, and put a foot on the trunk again.

Oliver was used to working with longer shoelaces, but laces were laces. In the split second that Bill's left foot passed within an inch or two of his right, his severed bootlaces reached out like snakes and knotted around one another.

There was a scream of rage from the base of the tree.

"If you leave, I'll let you go quietly!" shouted Oliver, with bravado he didn't feel.

He leaned over. Bill was getting up again. He had fallen down, thus revealing the primary flaw with keeping a knife in your teeth. The lower half of his face was a mask of blood.

Bill tore his shoes off and began climbing in bare feet. He clenched the knife in his teeth again, though.

*Proving, I suppose, that learning from your mistakes is something that happens to other people...*

Oliver considered his options. Two spells to work with.

He tried the shoelaces again. The laces of Bill's jerkin knotted across the chest, but the bandit didn't seem to notice.

Oliver took a deep breath and let it out through his nose. *"Pushme... pullme..."*

The target was obvious.

The knife in Bill's teeth began to shake and rattle violently. There was no finesse required. Oliver just banged on the blade with his invisible "foot" until Bill stopped climbing and wrenched the knife loose.

"Don't matter!" the bandit shouted. "Don't matter! I'll kill you with my bare hands, you freakish little wizard-rat!"

He stabbed the knife into the tree-trunk and grabbed for the next branch. He was less than five feet from Oliver now.

Oliver transferred his magical attention to the branch and began stomping on it. It was almost as heavy as the bar on the barn door had been, but at least he could see it, and with his hands on the bark, he felt as if he were touching it as well.

Bill clutched at the shaking branch and shook himself. "Don't... matter..." he panted.

*He's still climbing. My god, what does it take to stop him?*

The bandit grabbed for Oliver's branch. He slipped several times, but at last got a handhold.

Oliver abandoned magic in favor of stomping on Bill's fingers several times, very hard.

Bill snarled and got his other hand up on the branch.

He grabbed for Oliver's trouser leg, caught a handful of fabric and pulled. Oliver tore free and grabbed for the tree trunk to steady himself.

*He doesn't have to grab me; he just has to pull me off! At this height, I'll splash when I hit the ground!*

*"Pushme!"* yelled Oliver desperately, trying to get around the other side of the tree trunk. *"Pushme—pullme—!"*

He threw magic at Bill frantically, trying to repel him, trying to slow him—something! Down on the ground, the bandit's discarded shoelaces had to be tied up in a knot the size of a fist.

Bill got all the way onto the branch. He swung a fist at Oliver.

The blow missed, but Oliver felt the air whistle by his ear as he ducked.

The power was rising again, as it had before, when he tried to become invisible—but this time, Oliver didn't wait to feel it washing over him. He grabbed at it with his mind.

It was almost exactly like knocking a glass over with your elbow and grabbing for it before it hit the floor—except that it was mostly inside his head.

*Shoelaces!* he thought frantically.

There was a muffled cry from the other side of the trunk.

Oliver leaned over, ready to throw himself downward and hope to catch a branch on the way.

Bill's hair had come alive.

The thick, greasy locks had tied themselves together. Bill might not have noticed that—it probably wasn't the first mat in his hair—but the tangles were also tied to his beard and the laces on his jerkin.

As Oliver watched, Bill's jerkin began to pull itself up around his ears, dragged by the rapidly knotting laces. The sleeves split as he flailed at it.

Oliver had never tried pouring power into the shoelace spell before. It was so straightforward a spell that it would never had occurred to him to try.

He was trying now.

More! More! Tighter!

Bill's traitorous hair yanked the jerkin up over the bandit's eyes.

Oliver held his breath.

Bill reached for the shirt, tore at it—and lost his balance.

*"Pushme, pullme!"* screamed Oliver, switching spells so fast that he felt the familiar *crack* inside his head.

*Oh, that's gonna be a nosebleed...*

Bill fell.

Branches snapped. There was a flat, final *thud.* It didn't seem nearly loud enough to Oliver. Maybe the ringing in his ears was drowning it out.

Silence.

⚜

Oliver clung to the tree with his face pressed into the bark, breathing in wet, sobbing gasps. He knew that he should keep climbing up or climb down or something... he didn't know what, but *something,* not sitting here practically biting the bark off the tree to keep from screaming...

The armadillo called, "Come down around the other side of the tree."

The armadillo. Eglamarck. Yes. His familiar. His friend. Yes. Oliver took a steadying breath.

"Is he dead?" he asked.

The armadillo was silent for a moment, then repeated, "Come down around the other side of the tree," and Oliver knew.

He put his forehead against the damp trunk and breathed for a minute.

Then, because nothing would be gained by staying up the tree, he scrabbled downward until he reached the ground.

He could see one of Bill's boots. He carefully didn't look any higher. He'd seen a dead body before, but it had been the old wizard, and he'd been sitting in his chair, peacefully gone, not dead by violence.

"Are we—should we bury him?" he asked.

"We don't have time," said the armadillo. "The ghuls won't bury us if they catch us. Come on, hurry."

The armadillo was right. Oliver knew he was right. It just didn't *seem* right.

*But what else can I do?* Oliver couldn't give someone last rites, like a priest, and there weren't any sin-eaters around. Bill had probably had a lot more sins than anybody could choke down anyway.

For a mad moment, all he could think of was Vezzo slaughtering hogs. Oliver had helped many times—not with the slaughter, but scraping the bristles, which was a long, hot, tedious job that required four people working in shifts. When Vezzo did it, he was fast and kind. The hog would squeal once, in surprise, not pain, and then fall down and not move again. And then Vezzo would lay one of his big blood-stained farmer's hands on the hog's flank and say, "Thank you."

Oliver had seen him thank any number of pigs that way and every time, he would swear, the farmer meant it. He understood what he was taking, and he was grateful.

Bill's not a hog. That's not how it works. But I don't know what else I can do, and I have to do something!

Oliver took a deep breath. He walked around the tree and put his hand on Bill's shoe. The jerkin was still up over the bandit's face.

He said, "Thank you." It was the wrong thing to say, completely the wrong thing, but he didn't have any other words. All the other words would have been worse. His voice was very high, but it didn't crack. And then he followed the armadillo into the woods, looking for another place to hide.

"So here is my plan," said Oliver, a few hours later. "We lead the ghuls onto Stern's men, then in the confusion, you go and bite through Trebastion's ropes." He tried to think of something else to add, because this seemed very short for a proper plan. "Um. Then we run away."

"This is a terrible plan," said the armadillo. "The ghuls are faster than you are, and my teeth aren't made for sawing through ropes."

Oliver wanted to be offended, but in good conscience, he couldn't. "I know." He sagged. "It's the best I can come up with."

The armadillo nudged his hand with his snout. "And I can't think of a better one," he admitted.

"You can't?"

"No."

"Oh. Darn." Oliver had rather been hoping that the armadillo would have a brilliant idea, or at least one that didn't involve the ghuls. He felt very strange about leading the ghuls onto other people. It seemed much more wicked than having the pigs attack the bandits. Pigs were pigs. They were just something that happened, almost a natural disaster, like tornadoes or sinkholes. The ghuls were unnatural and evil.

He wouldn't mind if the ghuls ate Mayor Stern, but he wasn't sure how he'd feel if they hurt the other men. They had gone along with Stern, true, but they were more like the villagers back home than really evil. They were normal people roped into a bad business, that was all.

They watched Trebastion get beaten and they didn't stop it, he reminded himself.

*Yes, but is that really enough to merit getting attacked by flesh-eating monsters?*

"I can hear you dithering," said the armadillo.

Oliver sighed. "I'm having second thoughts," he admitted.

"You're well past second. Fourth or fifth by now, I'd say."

"This isn't *right.*"

"No," said the armadillo. He tapped his claws on a tree root. "We can still leave, you know. Call this whole thing a wash and go up to the Rainblades."

"We can't leave Trebastion!"

"Sure, we can," said the armadillo. "No one will stop us. No one will even know, except Trebastion, and he won't know for very long."

Oliver stared at him, horrified.

The armadillo snorted. "Well, there's your answer. No, it's not right. It's also not right to let your friend get slowly taken apart by Stern. But those men aren't going to stop him, which means that they're in our way."

It seemed to Oliver that things were more complicated than that, or at least they should be more complicated than that... and yet, the armadillo was right. It was that or leave Trebastion to be killed. Probably tortured to death.

"All right," he said wearily. "Where do we find the ghuls?"

❧

Finding the ghuls was easy. The armadillo thought privately that it was too easy, that the forest itself was rejecting the creatures, tearing at them with twigs and thorns, turning stones and branches underfoot. They left a trail nearly as wide as the pigs, stinking of too-sweet ghul-scent.

The thought seemed ridiculous on the face of it, but Hark-hound was not like other forests. The armadillo remembered that strange aftertaste, like a shadow on his tongue, and the flash of red that Oliver claimed to have seen. *Perhaps not so ridiculous after all.*

"Oliver?" he said, pausing in the middle of the trail, nostrils flared.

"Yeah?"

"Can you... ah..." He scuffed at his nose with his claws, embarrassed to be asking. "Tell the forest we're trying to get rid of them?"

To his wizard's credit, Oliver didn't argue. He just said "Okay, I'll try," and leaned against a tree. The armadillo could hear him thinking at the woods, like a conversation in the next room, although Oliver was so loud that he could make out the words anyway: WE'RE TRYING TO GET RID OF THE GHULS. CAN YOU HELP US?

That last bit was a good addition. Eglamarck wouldn't have thought of it. He'd have been content to ask the forest to stay out of their way. It came of being a social species, he supposed. Armadillos didn't often ask other armadillos for help.

Probably it was pointless. Probably the woods weren't that smart, or didn't speak human, or...

The taste of leafmould flooded his mouth, so strong and earthy that he nearly spat. Branches sighed overhead.

... or he was wrong.

Well, if Oliver was right and the ghost of the farmer's wife was haunting the woods, it stood to reason that human ghosts thought like humans, not like armadillos. Good enough.

"All right," he whispered. "We're clear on the plan?"

"Clear," whispered Oliver.

There was a very good chance that they were both going to die. Eglamarck knew this. He also knew that humans usually liked to say things under such circumstances, as if saying words might ward off death or make it more palatable. He waited.

A hand came down and rubbed between his ears. "You're a good familiar," Oliver whispered.

"You're a good wizard," said the armadillo gruffly. "Now go throw a rock at the ghuls and let's get this over with."

❦

Oliver crept within range of the ghuls. They were still awake, which he didn't like. It was close to dawn and they had bedded down, but he'd been hoping that they'd already be asleep. The extra few seconds as they woke up might be crucial.

Still, they didn't dare wait another day. Mayor Stern would move, probably several miles at least, and there was no way that Oliver could hope to lead the ghuls for miles. And Trebastion might not be able to take any more of Stern's abuse, even if they stayed in the same place.

Oliver screwed up his courage, picked up a rock, and flung it at the ghuls.

He didn't wait to see if he had hit one. He turned and sprinted away.

Querulous noises rose from the dark behind him. The Bryerlys—or whatever the Brylerlys had become—had definitely noticed the rock.

He didn't waste time. They were faster than he was, he was sure of it. His only advantage was surprise and an armadillo.

THEY'RE AFTER ME he thought, as loud as he could.

*The whole damn forest is after you by the sound of it,* came the acid reply.

He didn't have the breath to laugh, but he was amused anyway. Crashing noises came from the undergrowth, followed by a long string of inhuman syllables. The forest wasn't making it easy for the ghuls.

Oliver ran. Every step in the dark risked a broken leg or a broken neck, which was still probably preferable to what would happen if the ghuls caught him.

*You're almost at the hand-off,* the armadillo told him.

I AM? ALREADY? It hadn't felt like it. He felt as if he still had a lot of running left in him.

*Save it,* said the armadillo. *You'll need it later.*

Oliver nodded, forgetting his familiar couldn't see him, and dove under a set of bushes.

His heart was hammering in his ears and his lungs wanted to gasp for air, but he didn't dare. He forced himself to breathe shallowly, mouth open, even though he felt half-strangled.

The crashing sounds of the ghuls slowed as they approached.

"Where?" said one, in a thin waspish voice. "Where, where?"

"Shut up!" hissed the other one. "Listen!"

Oliver's nerves screamed. He heard twigs snapping. It seemed like they had to be mere inches away.

Then leaves rattled and he heard a thud, as if someone went floundering through the trees off to his left. The ghuls both inhaled sharply. "There!" one said, triumphant, and they charged in the direction of the sound.

THEY'RE HEADING YOUR WAY.

*They damn well better. I had to break a perfectly good rotten log for that, and I didn't even get to eat one grub.*

Oliver crawled out from under the bush and began to slink in the direction of Stern's campsite. The crashing noises were so loud that he was surprised Stern couldn't hear it.

He'd gotten perhaps a quarter of the way to the campsite when the armadillo spoke into his mind again. *Better get them off me. They've figured out I'm not a human and they're starting to hunt lower down.*

Oliver picked up a stick and swung it hard against a tree trunk two or three times, then broke into a run.

*That did it*, said the armadillo. *Heading your way now.*

The ghuls hadn't exactly sounded happy before, but now they sounded downright angry. "Someone is playing gamesss," hissed one of them. "Someone thinks they're *clever.*"

"Clever meat is sweeter," said the other one.

Oliver did not feel particularly clever. He kept his head down, trying to duck under as many branches as possible. He'd never much liked being short, but when your pursuers were six feet tall, it was a definite advantage.

He needed any advantage he could get. He was tiring more quickly now. A stitch was starting up in his side, jabbing him in the ribs with every breath.

GETTING TIRED, he admitted.

*You're nearly there*, said the armadillo. *Or I'm nearly there, as the case may be.*

A ghul squawked in alarm, far too close behind him. "That was my face!" it snarled.

"Should have ducked!"

Oliver took advantage of their squabbling to dive into a

tangle of logs. A moment later, the armadillo began to crash loudly through the woods and the ghuls were off once more.

It was a simple plan, ultimately. They lured the ghuls in a long zig-zag between them, and eventually onto Mayor Stern. For a minute, hidden in the logs, Oliver started to hope that it might work.

Then everything went bad.

*They've split up*, the armadillo thought. *I only hear one. Watch yourself.*

Oliver cursed silently. He couldn't remain still, though. He climbed to his feet and hurried toward the campsite, bent practically double, trying to keep his breathing quiet. The skin on the back of his neck crawled, expecting ghul claws to close over it at any moment.

He was almost to the last point where they were supposed to trade off when the armadillo thought, *Ah, hell.*

It was quiet, resigned, and it chilled Oliver to the bone. WHAT? WHAT?

*One got ahead of me. They've got me trapped.*

TRAPPED?

*Won't be long now, I'm afraid.*

ARMADILLO?

EGLAMARCK?

Nothing.

Oliver threw caution, plans, and everything else to the winds and charged toward the armadillo.

"Hold on!" he yelled, and realized he was yelling out loud as well as mentally, which probably wasn't helpful. He didn't even have a weapon against the ghuls, not so much as a pointy stick, but they had his familiar and that was the only thing that mattered.

*Don't be a fool*—the armadillo tried to say, and then Oliver burst between the trees and crashed headlong into a ghul.

The ghul fell down. Oliver almost fell over the top of it. In the gray light of pre-dawn, he could make out the second ghul blinking at him. It was holding something to its mouth, something the size and shape of a mostly rolled-up armadillo.

The ghul's mouth was open and it was *biting* his *familiar*.

All thoughts of magic went out of his mind. Oliver screamed in rage and punched the ghul in the stomach.

Surprise was definitely the only thing that saved him. The ghul let out a grunt and the armadillo, already hunched up in as tight a ball as he could manage, suddenly kicked free, dropping to the ground.

"You!" said the ghul. "You and your nasty scaled rat!"

*Run, you idiot!* yelled the armadillo. *Run! Behind you!*

Oliver bolted sideways. The second ghul's arms closed over empty air and it tripped over the armadillo and went down again. Oliver scrambled over a tree trunk and pelted through the woods, praying they followed him and didn't stop to grab the armadillo again.

*Don't worry about me! Run!*

He'd lost his sense of direction. Which way was the campsite? He should see the fire by now, but maybe it was getting too light, maybe the fire wouldn't stand out any longer, what if he was running in the wrong direction—

Red flared in the corner of his vision and swept behind a tree. Oliver changed direction and ran toward it, nearly sobbing with relief. His ghostly benefactor was back.

He burst out of the trees into Mayor Stern's campsite barely a step ahead of the ghuls. A dozen startled faces turned toward him.

"*Ghuls!*" bellowed Oliver.

"Wha—?" said someone and then the ghuls came out of the woods behind him.

Oliver had been a little afraid that the ghuls might talk to Stern. They were clearly capable of lying, and if they'd been very clever, they might have tried to claim that Oliver was a thief (or worse, their runaway son) and so retreat without bloodshed.

He needn't have worried. The ghuls saw a dozen humans—a dozen sources of *meat*—and reacted like feral dogs in a henhouse.

They went berserk.

Stern's men had been in the process of breaking the camp. One man was still holding a set of blankets in his arms when the first ghul leaped on him, biting at his face and grabbing at the back of his head with red-knuckled fingers. He went down. The ghul tore at his flesh, hissing in pleasure.

"What is going on here?!" roared Stern.

Oliver didn't wait to see what the second ghul had done. By the sound of the screams, it wasn't pretty. Trebastion knelt near the fire, hands tied behind him, face a mask of dried blood, and Oliver dashed toward him.

Stern swung around. "Get away from him!" he said—to Oliver, not the ghul. Oliver tied his shoelaces together with as much venom as he could muster.

Stern made two steps, hopped on one foot, and fell down with a roar of fury. One of the ghuls spotted him and leapt off the man it had been attacking, eyes shining with delight.

"Meat!" it sang. "Meat, lovely meat!"

One of Stern's men grabbed the mayor's elbow and hauled him to his feet. The ghul swayed back and forth in front of them, like a snake deciding whether to strike.

Oliver got an arm under Trebastion's shoulders and tried to pull him upright. "Come on!" he whispered. "Come on, you've got to move..."

"What the hell are those things?" whispered Trebastion. He sounded much more coherent than Oliver would have expected, given the abuse he'd been taking.

"Ghuls. Come on, come on, they're bad..."

"I got that!" Trebastion regained his footing, staggered, but managed to catch himself against Oliver. Oliver tried to steer the groggy minstrel toward the trees. The skin between his shoulder blades crawled. He was expecting a ghul or Stern to grab him at any moment. He looked over his shoulder, just in time to see the ghul stop its sway and lunge for Stern.

The mayor grabbed the man who had helped him to his feet and flung him into the ghul's embrace. The ghul rocked sideways, giggled, and wrapped its arms around the man. Despite all the yelling, Oliver heard, with horrible clarity, the sound of the ghul's teeth in the man's throat, a crisp wet crunch like a man biting into an apple.

It was all so sudden and shocking that Oliver could barely comprehend it. Surely, he couldn't have just seen the mayor throw one of his own men at the monsters to save his own skin. Surely...

The others saw it too.

A strange, low noise rose from a half-dozen throats. Oliver had never heard it before, but he recognized it instantly. It was one of the calls of the mob. It was a sound of horror and betrayal. It was the sound of men realizing they had been misled.

It frightened Oliver almost as much as the ghuls. A crowd making that sound would tear you apart just as easily as a ghul would, even if they didn't eat you afterward.

*Oh god what have I done oh god I brought the ghuls on them they're dying some of them are dead I didn't mean for this I knew it would happen, but I didn't know what it would be like...*

He knew that he should just run. He knew that the longer the men and ghuls fought, the better off he'd be. But he couldn't leave it. "Fire!" he shouted. "They're afraid of fire!"

For a moment it seemed like no one heard him. Then one of the men reached down and grabbed a log that was still smoldering in the fire and swung it at the nearest ghul. It leapt away, squalling and swearing, and the man pressed his advantage, driving it back from the flame.

*It's not enough, but it's all I can do.* "Come on," Oliver said to Trebastion, his voice cracking as if the words were a sob. "Come on, we have to get out of here..."

Stern took a halting step toward him. "Don't you dare run!" he snarled. "Get away from that boy!" Oliver didn't know if the man was talking to him or to Trebastion. It probably didn't matter either way.

Stern took another shuffling step. His bootlaces were a mass of knots and he could only move a few inches at a time.

Trebastion was moving like he was dead drunk. Oliver walked backwards behind him and Stern was much too close and Oliver thought, *this is the stupidest race I have ever run*, and over Stern's shoulder, one of the other men stabbed the ghul between the ribs with a knife.

Oliver wanted to cheer. The ghul howled, dropping his victim, and turned, but another man was there with a burning stick to drive it back.

Stern didn't even look around. He kept shuffling after Oliver and Trebastion, a creature from a nightmare, slow and relentless.

The armadillo hit him in the back of the knees, and he went down with a scream.

They were almost at the treeline. Trebastion nearly fell again but caught himself on a tree trunk. The armadillo scooted past them and Oliver could not resist one last look over his shoulder.

One of the ghuls was down. The second one was surrounded by a trio of men bearing torches. But two men were also standing over Stern, and their faces were cold and expressionless. Oliver's nerves screamed that the mayor could still turn it all around, still talk his way out of it, he only had to say the right thing.

"Get that fool minstrel!" he snarled, pushing himself to his feet. "Go after him, you idiots! He's getting away!"

That was not the right thing.

Oliver stepped back into the trees and left Mayor Stern and the ghuls to their fate.

## ❧ 10 ❧

I t took longer than anyone would like to get Trebastion's
ropes off. Oliver's knife was long gone to the bandits and
the armadillo really didn't have the teeth for it. "I don't
even have enamel," he said irritably. "You're better off gnawing it
yourself." But eventually they found a sharp rock and Trebastion
managed to wiggle them off, even though his hands were scraped
and raw by the end.

There was no sign of Stern or any of the men. Oliver
suspected that they had their own problems to deal with now,
but he was still glad that Trebastion had managed to get a fair
distance, even with his hands tied, before they had to stop. It
was full daylight now, and that made moving easier, but it also
meant that they could be spotted at a much greater range.

"How are you still walking?" asked Oliver, as Trebastion
finally got his hands in front of him. "I thought you were dying!"

Trebastion rolled his eyes. "If somebody's beating you, you go
limp and pretend to be much worse off than you are," he said.
"Otherwise they keep beating on you. I've felt a lot better, but I
wasn't going to give Stern an excuse to keep going."

Oliver nodded, tossing the sharp rock down, and turned.

And stopped.

"Let's get the hell out of here," said Trebastion behind him. "I never want to see this forest again."

"I don't think we can," said Oliver. "Not just yet."

"What?"

Oliver pointed.

There were only a few threads hanging on the branch, but they were brilliant, ripe-tomato red. Trebastion's eyes nearly crossed as he focused on them. "Huh…?"

"I think it's the farmer's wife," said Oliver. "From your song." He looked past the threads and for an instant, thought he saw a flicker of red in the trees. "She helped us before. I couldn't have rescued you without her."

"But that was just a song!" Trebastion insisted.

"You told me that old timers said it had really happened."

"Yeah, but they say that about everything! They say that about the song with the mad bull and the maiden, and everybody's grandfather supposedly knew somebody in the next town over from the miller with the bloody millstone!"

Oliver shrugged. "Come on," he said, heading in the direction of the flash of red. "I think she wants something."

"But what do ghosts want?"

"Don't look at me," said the armadillo, trotting after Oliver. "I can't see red anyway."

Trebastion gripped his head in both hands, muttering to himself, and then followed after the armadillo and the very minor mage.

❦

The ghost of the farmer's wife—Oliver wished the song had included her name, since it didn't seem fair to keep thinking of her in terms of the person who had indirectly murdered her—led them northwest, into a part of the forest they hadn't seen before. The trees here were very tall, a vaulted cathedral of green. Ferns had nestled into cracks in the bark and hung down in long chains.

Every few hundred yards, there was another red thread caught on a twig or draped over a fern.

"Where is she taking us?" whispered Trebastion.

"I don't know," Oliver whispered back. It did not seem right to speak loudly, as if they were in a church or attending a funeral. "Can you see her? Not just the threads?"

"I see... something." He rubbed his eyes. "Not directly, but I keep getting little flashes."

Oliver nodded. He deliberately hadn't looked behind him to see if the threads were vanishing as they passed. He didn't know whether it would be better or worse if they were.

"If it wasn't for the threads, I'd think my eyes were just tired," admitted Trebastion.

"You're not," said the armadillo. "There's something there."

"Can you see her?"

The armadillo gave him a wry look. "I can barely see *you*. No, I smell something. There's an aftertaste to the air here. Could be a ghost. Could be Harkhound itself. This forest is more than just the trees."

"Heads up," said Oliver, stopping in his tracks. "I think we're getting there. Wherever *there* is." He nodded to a gap in the trees. "She's standing still."

Trebastion blinked repeatedly, moving his head back and forth rather like the armadillo hunting a slug. "Where... ah, yeah, there."

They waited silently. Oliver slowly turned his head, trying to bring the bit of red into better focus.

She was not young. That surprised him. He had been picturing a young woman for some reason, probably because of the romance of the ballad. Instead she was his mother's age, her hair streaked with gray. She stood in the gap between two large trees, smoothing her apron down with her hands.

I've faced ghuls and bandits and Mayor Stern, Oliver told himself. A ghost is nothing. A well-intentioned ghost, no less.

He took a step forward. The ghost did not fade as he approached. She kept her hands in her apron, eyes downcast.

"Hello," said Oliver finally.

The ghost glanced up, then back down.

"You've... um... been very helpful. I'm very grateful."

Another glance up and down.

"I'm grateful too," said Trebastion. "I hear you saved my bacon, ma'am." He bowed to the ghost very deeply, his arms out to one side in a minstrel's flourish.

A fleeting smile crossed the ghost's face. *A ghost of a smile,* thought Oliver, and then was immediately grateful that the armadillo hadn't heard that thought, because he'd probably get nipped in the shins.

The four of them stood there—mage, minstrel, armadillo and ghost—for a moment that stretched on and on. Oliver wondered what he was supposed to do next, if anything.

The ghost seemed to come to some decision at last, because she stepped aside and stretched a hand out to point through the gap.

"All right," said Oliver. He took a deep breath and stepped forward.

*Go on. It's okay to turn your back on her. She's a ghost, she can just pop up behind you any time she wants.* His skin prickled anyway, but he kept his eyes firmly forward.

There was coolness to the air on his right, where the ghost stood, like the mist from a waterfall on a warm day. Then he was through the gap and looking down into a little hollow formed by the roots of the trees.

The hollow was full of bones.

Oliver had expected that, honestly. It made sense. He spent a nervous moment checking for extra skulls, just in case the farmer's wife had been luring travelers here to murder them, but there was only one. *And it's not as if she didn't have plenty of opportunity to see us dead before now.*

Scavengers had disturbed the bones, but most still seemed to be present. Rags of cloth were still draped over them, long faded by rain and rot.

"Oh, hell," muttered Trebastion behind him.

"It's her grave," said Oliver.

"No," said Trebastion. "It's her bones. She doesn't have a grave. Nobody buried her."

From the corner of her eye, Oliver saw the farmer's wife nodding.

"Do you think that's what she wants?" asked Oliver softly.

Trebastion nodded. "It's what most of them want," he said. "That and justice. But I think it's been so long now that justice is off the table."

The ghost nodded again, a rueful expression crossing her face.

"Let me," said Trebastion. "I've got some experience with handling skeletons."

He knelt down beside the bones. His long fingers were surprisingly gentle as he straightened out the jumble of bone. The ancient rags fell apart as he touched them. Had they been red once? Oliver could not tell.

*I hope he doesn't feel like he has to make a harp out of it.*

Fortunately, he did not. He moved the bones into a rough human shape, setting the skull into place on a pillow of moss.

The ghost watched intently as he worked. Oliver kept watch out of the corner of his eyes. She'd been benevolent so far, but what if she was expecting a blood sacrifice or something?

Trebastion finished his job and pulled his coat off. He glanced at Oliver. "You say she saved me?"

This did not seem like the time to argue that it had been a joint effort. Oliver nodded.

Trebastion laid the coat reverently over the skeleton, tucking it in around the collarbone. He sat back on his heels and began to sing.


In the trees, in the trees
   Her spirit still walks
   In her kirtle of red
   In the trees, in the trees, in the trees


Trebastion nodded. He picked up two sticks and cut a strip off the bottom of his already ragged shirt, tying it together into a crude cross for a headstone.

By the time he had finished, there were only three of them left in the hollow with her bones.

"I hope your song isn't accurate any longer," said Oliver, as they left the grave.

"Me, too," said Trebastion. He scrubbed at his face with his hands. "I wish I'd known her name."

"Do you think she died from the smoke?"

"No." Trebastion shook his head. "One of her leg bones was broken. I don't think it was scavengers, or they'd have dragged it away. I think she probably broke her leg, and no one was here to help her."

Oliver glanced back over his shoulder, at the gap in the trees slowly vanishing behind fern and bark. "So, she decided to help people who needed it."

Trebastion nodded. "There's a lot of songs about people who go the other way and start trying to punish everybody who didn't help them."

"Which probably proves that ghosts are like everyone else," said the armadillo. He flicked his tail against Oliver's shins. "Come on. We're not far from the foothills now, I don't think. I can smell open spaces."

## ❧ 11 ❧

The armadillo's nose proved accurate. The way got steeper, going up, and the trees began to thin out. By mid-day, they were standing on a weedy slope, looking down at the forest.

Oliver had never been so glad to see emptiness. He wanted to run around with his arms out, for the sheer novelty of not running into anything. Trebastion let out a whoop and did a little dance. The armadillo vanished into a thicket of pokeweed, then re-emerged, licking his lips.

"I never want to go into a forest again," said Trebastion. "I am *done* with forests. Forests are now off my list for the foreseeable future."

Oliver gazed up the slope. He hadn't really given any thought to where in the Rainblades he was going. The Cloud Herders lived here somewhere, according to the old wizard, but he hadn't been more specific than that.

A child of lowlands, it had not really occurred to Oliver that mountains were very large and a whole mountain range was larger yet. When he looked up, he saw stony cliffs and steep hillsides draped in green, but no people.

"Now where do we go?" he muttered.

The armadillo heard him and came trotting. "I suggest we follow the smell of sheep."

"Sheep?"

"There's old sheep dung here." The armadillo scuffed at the ground with a claw. "A fair amount but dried out. If you've got sheep, you've got shepherds. We just have to find where the sheep are, and we'll find the shepherd."

"You think the shepherd will be one of the Cloud Herders?"

The armadillo shrugged. "Maybe, maybe not. I do think that if you've got magic people who control the rains living in the area, anyone local will probably know where they are. For self-preservation, if nothing else."

Oliver considered this and had to admit that it was a good idea. Everybody in the surrounding towns had known where the old wizard lived, and there was only one of him. "Can you smell where they went?"

"I'm an armadillo, not a bloodhound." The armadillo began to pick his way up the slope. "I suggest we start walking and look for sheep."

৩৫৯

It took another day to find signs of sheep. They stuck to the edge of Harkhound in case they had to duck into the forest again. As little as any of them wanted to spend more time in the trees, Oliver had to admit that the steep slopes of the Rainblades were not a place he'd want to wait out a storm. The wind made sleeping on the hillside a chilly prospect, so they kept the green line of Harkhound in view.

Twice they saw animals at a distance and got excited, before discovering that the creatures were mountain goats. They were handsome animals with short black horns, but they did not belong to anyone except themselves.

Oliver spent the long hours replaying that moment in his head when he had tied Stern's shoelaces together.

It was such a strange thing to fixate on. He knew that. He should be thinking about the men who had died. But somehow it was this one moment that kept rattling around in his head, like a dried pea in a bowl.

He hadn't thought about it. He'd just done it. *And I'd do it again. Of course, I would. He was bad. He was a murderer who sacrificed his own people to the ghul.*

He didn't feel guilty about it, not like he had with Bill, or even the men who the ghuls had killed. But it still seemed to him that he *should* have thought before he did it. He knew he could kill people. He knew that the spell might be a death sentence with the ghuls there. And yet he hadn't thought at all.

*There should have been a moment when I stopped and thought and knew what I was doing and thought about the consequences. Shouldn't there?*

Adults always told you to stop and think about what you were doing. Oliver hadn't thought. He hadn't had time to think. It was a man's life hanging on that spell and he *knew* it was a man's life and yet he hadn't thought at all.

*If you knew that someone might die if you did something, shouldn't you think about it first? Even for just a moment?*

*It worked out,* said the armadillo in his head.

*What if it hadn't?*

*Humans. You beat yourselves up for failure and you beat yourselves up almost as bad for success. Feh.*

Possibly that was the only thing to be said about the matter, but Oliver could not help worrying at it like a sore tooth.

It was approaching mid-afternoon on the second day when Trebastion pointed and said, "Are those more goats?"

Oliver followed the line of his arm to a dozen small white shapes. They looked different than the goats, but it was hard to tell from such a distance. "Maybe?" He rubbed his lower back. Walking on the uneven slope for hours was leaving him sore in unexpected places. Having sore knees and hips made him feel strangely old.

They scrambled across the slopes toward the potential sheep. The hills were not smooth but folded up in odd places, so that they often had to go hundreds of yards out of their way to get somewhere comparatively close at hand. It took a long time and they were both short of breath. Oliver had to stop and pick up the armadillo several times.

Sheep glanced up incuriously at their approach. They were much whiter and softer looking than the ratty cream-colored sheep Oliver was used to. A ram with spiraled horns and deep gray streaks stood out from the rest like a storm cloud. All of them had wispy white feathering on the back of their legs like draft horses.

"Those are sheep, all right," said Oliver. "Now we just need to figure out where the shepherd is."

Someone cleared his throat loudly. The armadillo sighed.

The shepherd leaned against a stone, not so much hidden as extraordinarily still. He was tall and tan-skinned, with a lean face and thick white hair. He did not look old, despite the color of his hair, but that was not the most extraordinary thing about him.

He was covered in swirling lines, tattooed or painted, Oliver could not tell, and the lines glowed brilliant blue, the color of a summer sky.

"Damn..." breathed Trebastion. "Will you look at that?"

Oliver's vision of mystical figures standing atop a stone did not quite mesh with the man in front of him, and yet... *He's a herder, and those tattoos are definitely magic.* The man's aura was a thread of vibrant blue light.

"Are you a Cloud Herder?" asked Oliver.

The man inclined his head.

Oliver glanced over at the sheep. They looked puffy and white, like clouds, but they were most definitely sheep. He felt a sudden stab of alarm. *What if they don't know anything about the rains? Everybody in Loosestrife just knew that the Cloud Herders controlled the rain, but it's not in any of my books. What if this is one of the things the old wizard didn't explain?*

The Cloud Herder said, "You are far from home."

"Yes," answered Oliver. "Um... hello?"

The Cloud Herder paused, perhaps puzzled by the conversation happening out of order, or perhaps simply amused. He nodded. "What brings you here?"

"I came to get rain," said Oliver, bracing himself for disappointment if the man said, "What does that have to do with me?"

The Cloud Herder's expression did not change, though the blue lines around his mouth seemed to pulse slightly. "You want us to send our clouds to pasture in your skies?"

That sounds... promising? At least he's acting like it's possible?

"Yes, please," said Oliver.

"Why?"

Oliver swallowed. "Err... because we need them?"

"Do you?"

"Yes. Very much. Um. The drought is very bad right now. People are going to die."

"Death comes to all people in time," said the Cloud Herder.

Oliver had no idea what to say to that. He hadn't expected to have to have this conversation quite so quickly, and he didn't know how to explain to this tall, blue-slashed man that he should care that people were suffering, that it *mattered* and he could fix it and if you could fix things, you should because otherwise there was no point to anything, you might as well just be ghuls or people like Mayor Stern.

He squared his shoulders and opened his mouth and the Cloud Herder held up his hand. "Enough."

"But—"

"I will take you to the Rain Wife. Plead your case to her, not me."

Oliver licked dry lips and nodded.

Oliver knew cattle better than sheep, but he was surprised to see that the Cloud Herder was willing to walk away from his flock. Then the painted man whistled and one of the largest shaggy white shapes separated itself from the flock and jogged toward him.

It was a dog. It had heavy jowls and a great ruff like a lion's mane. There were three glowing blue lines in its left ear. Oliver wondered if they were to identify the dog as belonging to this particular Herder or if there was something else about them.

"Watch them," said the Cloud Herder to the dog.

The dog sat down. Its gaze was sharper than any dog Oliver had ever met. A familiar, like Eglamarck? His own familiar was keeping well back, ears flicking worriedly.

The Cloud Herder turned and walked away. Oliver and Trebastion hurried after him.

The Cloud Herder village was not far away, though Oliver did not see it until they were nearly on top of it. The buildings were complicated structures of felted wool and weathered gray wood, nearly the same color as the hillside. They looked like flowers or folded paper, with multiple angled roofs and eaves. Smoke drifted from narrow chimneys and was lost in the white sky overhead.

It was a quiet place. Oliver nearly overlooked the people the first time, and then wondered how you could possibly overlook someone six feet tall and covered in glowing blue lines. And yet they moved quietly, and their voices were quiet and when he spotted someone, even if they were sitting in plain sight, it was a shock.

He counted half a dozen of the Cloud Herders, sitting on the front steps of the houses. Most of them carried drop spindles and it was by those small motions that his eyes were first attracted to them. Two children sat on the ground beside one of the buildings, playing a game that looked like marbles, but even their voices seemed muffled, as if they were a long way off.

"Forgive me," said Trebastion, walking beside the Herder, "but... ah... those glowing lines... how did you *do* that?"

His voice seemed very loud. For the first time, though, the Herder smiled. "It is the cloud milk," he said. "We tattoo ourselves with it."

Oliver glanced around. All the adults were heavily tattooed with the ink. The two children had blue dots on each cheek.

"I bet you never have any trouble finding keyholes at night," said Trebastion, clearly envious.

"There is enough darkness in the world," said the Herder. "We do not add to it unless we must."

He stopped before the tallest of the structures and gestured them inside. The drape over the doorway was heavy woven cloth, pale gray and rough against Oliver's fingers.

The interior of the building was lit by lanterns filled with the glowing blue cloud milk. Oliver wondered if they were literally milking clouds—which, at this point, was not even the strangest thing he had heard of—or if it was some other substance simply called cloud milk. Then he caught sight of the Rain Wife, sitting at the far end, and stopped thinking about anything else at all.

She was very fat, and her face was round, with heavy jowls like the dog on the hillside. Blue ink spiraled across the backs of her hands and down her forehead. Her aura burned like a brand in the dark. Despite the smoothness of her skin, he guessed from the lines around her eyes that she was very old.

They were lines of laughter, not sorrow, and Oliver dared to hope for a moment, but his eyes were caught by the enormous shape behind her.

It, too, was a face, but a woven one, at least five feet high. It had a suggestion of nose and ears, but no eyes or mouth. Then the Rain Wife raised her hand, and shapes suddenly scurried down from the ceiling and onto the woven face, forming the eyes and mouth and eyebrows.

"Welcome, young mage," said the Rain Wife.

The scurrying shapes rearranged themselves in long lines so that the face smiled, and the eyes squeezed up.

"Oh, damn," whispered Trebastion, "they're spiders."

"Does that surprise you?" asked the Rain Wife, clearly amused. "We are both weavers. And spiders and rain go together, you know."

"If you kill a spider, it will rain," said Oliver, through dry lips.

"So, they say. But it has not worked for your people, has it, young mage? That is why you have come, is it not?"

"Yes," said Oliver, tearing his eyes away from the spiders. "Yes, it is. There's been a drought."

"So, you came here, to ask for rain."

"Yes."

On the wall, the face showed its teeth in a laugh. Oliver stared at it, a detached part of his mind admiring how it was done. There were a dozen types, from very small, dark ones to big yellow-and-black ones as big as Oliver's hand. The largest spiders were extending their long front legs, making a dark U-shape outline around each tooth, while their bodies formed the darkness inside the mouth. It was really quite impressive, except for the bit where his skin was trying to crawl off his body.

"You're a mage," he said. "Aren't you? And those spiders..."

"My familiars," said the Rain Wife. "Like your scaled friend there." The spiders grinned at the armadillo. "I suspect that you would consider most of my people mages, in fact, though few of them are terribly powerful by an outsider's standards."

"I'm not very powerful either," Oliver admitted. Maybe that was foolish to admit, but he suspected that it would be far more foolish to try to lie to the Rain Wife.

"Powerful enough to have made it through Harkhound," said the Rain Wife. "That place is not patient with weakness."

"I think we were lucky," said Oliver.

The face laughed again.

"Luck is worth something." She shrugged. "Well, then. To

business. What will you give me, young mage?" asked the Rain Wife. "To give you the rains?"

Oliver's heart sank. Of course, the Cloud Herders wanted something. Everyone wanted something. Rain had to be incredibly valuable, didn't it? People would die without it. And here he had come, stumbling and foolish, without jewels or gold, with only a handful of copper coins, thinking that merely asking would be enough.

He squared his shoulders. "I have a little money," he said. "Not much."

"The rains cannot be bought with wealth," said the Rain Wife, while the spiders scurried into a stern expression behind her head. "Rich men die without water, the same as everyone else."

Oliver bit his lip. Had he offended her? Had he failed? Had he come all this way, only to accidentally insult the Rain Wife and ruin everything? "I'm sorry," he said. "My predecessor... he taught me everything... he didn't tell me what to do here. If there was something I should bring."

She tilted her head to one side, studying him. The spiders arranged themselves into a thoughtful stillness.

"Your mind is jumbled," said the Rain Wife at last. "Your thoughts tangle together like uncarded wool."

*Oh boy*, he heard the armadillo think. *If we have to wait until a human's thoughts are untangled, we'll die of old age before we get the rains back.* Which was not polite, but also not wrong. Oliver's heart, already in his toes, sank into the stony ground under his feet.

The Rain Wife laughed. The sound was unexpectedly musical, like water trickling over stones. "No, small one," she said to the armadillo, "we need not wait so long as that."

"You're reading my mind!" breathed the armadillo.

"Only the very top of it," said the Rain Wife. "Only the thoughts that might become words." She spread her hands. There were blue spirals on her palms that ran up her forearms and became blue deer with interlocking antlers that looked at Oliver with blank blue eyes. Behind her head, the spiders smiled, and their legs formed laugh lines. "Enough to see, mage, that you are young, and your thoughts are young and tangled."

"I am tired of being young," said Oliver, because he was thinking it loudly enough that it probably didn't matter if he said it out loud. "It didn't matter that I was young, my village sent me anyway." And he still resented that, but love and pity and resentment were all mixed together and he didn't have any way to untangle them.

"Yes," agreed the Rain Wife. "That is the price your village paid. You will never love them with your whole heart again. The shadow of what they did in their fear will lie between you forever. But they will be alive, nonetheless, and learning to bridge that shadow—or decide not to—is the work of adulthood."

Oliver bowed his head, wondering if he would ever be old enough for that. *Though I do miss Vezzo and Matty. And my mother.* He wondered when he had grown old enough that he was no longer embarrassed that he missed his mother.

The Rain Wife drummed her fingers on the arm of her chair. Oliver could hear another, softer tapping, and he hoped very much that it was an echo, and not the sound of dozens of spiders tapping their feet. "Will you give me your magic?" she asked suddenly.

"Err... what?" said Oliver.

"Your magic," said the Rain Wife. "In return for the rain." She must have read his puzzled expression, because she lifted one blue-painted hand and waved it negligently. "It's easy enough. I can spin it out of you, like spinning thread from wool. It would be gone, and you would be normal."

The thought was so bizarre and unexpected that he could only stare at her. Give up his magic? All of it? No longer be even the most minor of mages?

"You'd be normal," she said. "Like all the other boys. That's what you've always wanted, isn't it? To be normal?"

Oliver blinked at her. "N-no? Why would I want *that?*"

The Rain Wife gazed at him for a long moment, then burst out laughing. She had a deep, husky laugh. On the woven face, the spiders roared with silent amusement. "I stand corrected, young man," she said, wiping her eyes. "And thank you. At my age, sometimes you start to think you know how everything works already. It is nice to be put in my place from time to time. So, your magic is not a trauma and a torment for you, is it?"

"No," said Oliver. "I mean, I fix things..." His mind was a jumble of the Jenson boy with his swollen eyes and the gremlin-magic in the mill gears and all the other small problems that he was able to fix for people. It was useful. He hoped the Rain Wife could pull that out of his mind, because if he tried to explain it, he was afraid he'd sound like he was bragging. He had a feeling that this woman would not be very impressed with bragging.

"Would you give that up for rain?"

Oliver's heart, which he'd thought could sink no lower, seemed to plunge to the center of the earth.

Give up his magic? Trade this one great act for all the things he might do, forever after?

You have to help people if they're suffering.

But if he had no magic, he couldn't help people, could he? I mean, obviously I can, I can like... I don't know, do their laundry or something, but I can't fix things like the Jenson boy's poison ivy or the mischief in the mill. It was easy to say that one person could always make a difference, but it was certainly a lot easier to make one if you had the ability to command arcane forces, even extremely minor ones.

But it won't matter if I can cure poison ivy if no one has rain. They'll die.

The armadillo crept closer and leaned against his shins. Oliver had a sudden sickening realization—if he had no magic, he'd have no familiar. And Eglamarck was his best friend.

Could he really trade his best friend away? Even with the whole village at stake?

No. The village had traded *him* for rain, and he was fairly certain, on some deep level, that was a wound that would scar over but never heal. He couldn't turn around and do it to someone else.

"I can't," he said. "I can't. I would, but..." He shook his head. The words wouldn't come, or there were too many of them and he was afraid that they'd come all at once and he might start crying. He didn't want to cry in front of the Rain Wife and Trebastion.

The armadillo turned his narrow head and sighed.

"No, you can't," said Trebastion. Oliver jumped a little. He'd completely forgotten the minstrel was there.

Trebastion stepped forward until he was almost toe to toe with the Rain Wife. "Don't take his. He needs it. You can take mine instead."

Oliver stared at the back of Trebastion's head. "Really?" he said.

"Really?" said the Rain Wife. Her eyes lingered on the bruises across his face.

"My magic's never done anything but ruin my life," said Trebastion. "But Oliver here saved me. I'll give it to you if you give him rain for his village."

The Rain Wife's eyes lidded as she thought. Over her head, the spiders flashed through a dozen emotions in rapid succession —surprise, calculation, amusement, and more.

"Yes," she said. "Yes, I will agree to that." She smiled toothily. "It is less than I should take, but you have both surprised me today, and for that, I will take a little less. Astonishment keeps a person young." She stretched out a hand. "Give me your wrist."

Trebastion glanced nervously at the spiders above her head but held out his arm.

"You don't have to do this," said Oliver. "You really don't."

"Well, I'm going to," said Trebastion.

"But—"

"Oliver, shut up and let me do something useful with my magic for once."

The Rain Wife's face softened. "It won't hurt much," she said gently. "But you might want to close your eyes. People find this... unsettling."

Trebastion squeezed his eyes shut. Oliver wanted to look away, but professional curiosity kept him watching. He'd never known someone could take away someone else's magic. How was it done?

She held up a hand behind her and several large black-and-yellow spiders scuttled onto her hand from the woven face. She lowered them to Trebastion's arm. "A little pinch, now," she said. "I apologize, youngster. You, I think, have had enough pain to last you a long time."

Trebastion said, "Heh." Then he winced as she flicked her hand and a thin skein of blood began to roll down from his wrist.

The spiders descended on it. Oliver's immediate thought was that they were going to begin to feed and he felt ill. But the reality, as it turned out, was different.

They began to weave.

Trebastion's blood dyed their web—or perhaps they were weaving the blood itself into long lines of silk. Oliver did not know and could not guess. They worked busily, their threads crossing and interweaving, and a thin, ladder-like web began to drop from the minstrel's wrist toward the floor. The rungs of the ladder ran back and forth erratically, forming a shape that looked almost like writing.

Oliver squinted. The strands were much thicker than any web he'd ever seen, and the longer he looked, the more he was convinced that there really were words written in the rungs, but in an alphabet he did not know. He glanced at the Rain Wife, who was still holding Trebastion's hand. "Is that...?"

"In the old language of spiders," she said. "No, I can't read it either. My small friends try to translate, but there are things that

I suspect mammals are not meant to know." She smiled crookedly, looking down at the length of red web.

It was only a few inches from the ground when the Rain Wife said, "Enough," and put her thumb over the wound. The spiders hastily finished their work, tying off the ends. The largest arachnid lifted the web in its forelegs and offered it ceremoniously to the Rain Wife.

"Put your thumb where mine is, youngster," she said. Trebastion blinked at her, then hurried to comply. "It will stop bleeding in a few minutes. Cobweb is the finest of bandages, believe it or not."

"I believe you," said Trebastion. "Is that it? Is the magic... gone?"

The Rain Wife took the red web from her familiar's legs and draped it along her arm. The glowing blue blazed up, turning into a web of violet... and then the red web was gone and the blue slowly returned to normal. "It's gone," she assured Trebastion.

Trebastion's eyes closed in unutterable relief.

The Rain Wife glanced over at Oliver and smiled. "Does it frighten you?" she asked.

"Yes," said Oliver.

"Good. It should. It frightened me; the first time I saw it done. But you have earned your chance at rain." She pushed herself to her feet, picking up a cane from one side of the chair. Three yellow spiders made golden ornaments in her hair. "Open your eyes, young man, and let's see this through."

## ❧ 12 ❧

T rebastion stumbled a bit as they left the building. Oliver grabbed for him, but the Rain Wife was quicker, holding him up with one heavy arm and supporting them both on her cane. "Young man, I think you had best stay with us for a little while."

"Is it the magic?" asked Oliver. "Or the lack of magic, I guess?"

"No," said the Rain Wife, "it's the fact that he's got at least three bruised ribs, unless I miss my guess."

Trebastion managed a smile. "They weren't so bad," he said. "Until last night. Sleeping on the ground, you know."

"We'll put you on a bed of cloud wool," said the Rain Wife. "Could use some salve for those bruises, too. Someone took a dislike to you, did they?"

"A man named Stern," said Trebastion. "I may possibly have uncovered the fact he was murdering little girls."

"That'd do it, I expect. He still after you?"

"I don't think so, no. I think a ghul ate him."

"These things happen." She glanced at him and made a grumbling sound in her throat. "You need feeding, too. We'll put some meat on your ribs."

Trebastion ducked his head, smiling. Oliver was reminded of what he'd said in the forest, about a certain type of woman who always wanted to feed him.

The Rain Wife looked over at the tall Cloud Herder who had brought them in. "Gregor? Your flock's nearly due for shearing, but that's an observation, not an order. You've got a new babe at home, and I'll go ask Holly if it's too much trouble."

Gregor tilted his head to one side. The blue light pulsed in his face. "I will see it through," he said. "They found me, after all."

"You certain?"

The tall man glanced at Oliver. "His people need the rain. We've enough put by for now."

"I'll do my best to see you don't suffer by it," said the Rain Wife, nodding. "All right, young mage. Gregor will let you take his clouds."

It had not occurred to Oliver that the Cloud Herders might actually rely on their clouds the way that shepherds relied on sheep. Clouds were clouds, weren't they? And yet the way that the two Herders were talking, they sounded more like animals, and if so, Oliver was asking for a lot.

He looked up into the sky, which was vague and gray and undifferentiated. It was all cloud. How did this work?

They retraced their steps up the hillside. The Rain Wife leaned heavily on her cane, but did not seem to be slowed down at all. Once or twice she even caught Trebastion as he staggered.

At last they stood facing the flock of sheep that Oliver and Trebastion had spotted only an hour or two before. "Well, then," said the Cloud Herder. He jerked his chin in the direction of the flock. "There's the clouds, if you can ride the ram."

Oliver looked from the man to the sheep to the gray ram and said, "Um?"

The Rain Wife chuckled. She took a waterskin from her belt and squirted a few drops into her palm. The liquid glowed watery blue. She dipped her thumb in it and turned to Trebastion. "Close your eyes."

He obeyed. She smeared her thumb across his eyelids, then turned to Oliver.

Oliver closed his eyes obediently as she approached. He was still wary, but since Trebastion did not fall down screaming, presumably it was safe enough. Her thumb was warm and the blue liquid—cloud milk?—left a trail of dampness across his eyelids.

He opened his eyes again, as the Rain Wife used her cane to hitch herself down and offer the same treatment to the armadillo.

"Oh," said Trebastion. "Oh, I see." Oliver blinked several times.

Oh.

If clouds came to earth and grazed on hillsides... no, that wasn't right. Clouds obviously *had* come to earth to graze on the hillsides. Oliver was looking at them.

They still looked like sheep, more or less. But the sight the cloud milk gave him showed Oliver the truth. Their features shifted like clouds in the wind and sometimes they had more legs and sometimes rather less. He watched one turn around, not by turning but by simply pulling its head back into its wool and having it extrude on the other side of its body.

And the ram... the ram was a storm cloud. Lightning crawled along his horns and his eyes glowed the same electric blue as the Cloud Herder's tattoos. The long feathery hairs on the backs of his legs streamed in the wind, bits breaking off and fading away into mist.

Oliver gulped.

"I'm supposed to ride... *him?*"

The Rain Wife nodded. "Get up on his back and the flock will follow. Ride him over the sky to the village, and they'll rain for you. But then you must release him so that he can lead them back." She jerked her head toward Gregor. "It's his season's shearing of rain that you've bought, but no amount of magic will buy the clouds themselves."

"That's all right," said Oliver, rubbing his palms on his trousers. The ram eyed him in an unfriendly fashion. "I... uh... All right. Nice sheep?"

He took two steps forward and the ram lowered his head and charged.

Oliver dove out of the way with a yelp, bruising his shoulder on the stony ground. "I don't think he wants to be ridden!"

"You'll have to wrestle him down, I expect," said Gregor. "He's a fierce one."

"Wrestle him down?!"

Gregor untied a piece of knotted rope from his waist and tossed it to Oliver. It looked—and felt—like a faded halter. Even with his cloud milk enhanced vision, Oliver couldn't see anything special about it. "Is it magic?" he asked.

"No, it's rope," said Gregor.

The ram pawed the ground, glaring at Oliver with those brilliant blue eyes. His scalp felt strange and he lifted his hand to discover that his hair was standing on end.

The ram charged again. Oliver leapt out of the way again. He was pretty sure that the only reason he didn't get trampled that time was because the ram had to pull up short so as not to run into the Rain Wife, which he seemed unwilling to do.

"Is there some trick to this?" he asked, scrambling to the safety of the Rain Wife's feet. The ram paced back and forth, like something far more predatory than a sheep.

She raised an eyebrow. "No trick. How did you survive the trip here, anyway?"

"Mostly by tying people's shoelaces together and asking for help!" Oh, if only he could have become invisible! He could have snuck up on the ram, jumped on his back, and... and... well, he'd still have to get the halter over his head and then ride the blasted beast, but at least he'd been farther along than he was now.

"Armadillo?" he asked. "Can you talk to him?"

"I have been," said the armadillo. "It's mostly swearing. He's got a remarkable vocabulary, for a sheep." Gregor made a noise suspiciously like a laugh. The Rain Wife did laugh, thumping her cane on the ground.

"He thinks you're after his ladies," said the armadillo. "I suppose he's not wrong."

"His owner said I could!"

"I don't think," said the armadillo, as Oliver flung himself out of the way of another charge, "that he's in the mood for a complex discussion of personal autonomy and property rights."

Oliver groaned. *All right*, he thought. *All right. Stop reacting and think.*

"*Pushme pullme,*" he said under his breath, and tried to shove a magical foot in the ram's way.

The cloud ram tripped over it, just as he'd hoped, stumbled... and instead of falling, caught himself with a pair of legs that hadn't been there a few seconds earlier. He hopped awkwardly as his back legs became his front legs and vice versa but didn't lose his footing.

Oh hell. How do you trip an animal that can just move its legs around its body?

"Hard to knock down a cloud," said Gregor laconically.

"*Pushme pullme,*" growled Oliver, "*pushme pullme!*" He could feel a headache starting up, although whether from the magic or from bashing his head against the ground, he wasn't quite sure.

The ram gave another awkward hop, eyes fixed on Oliver. The mage had a feeling that once the ram got a clear shot at him, he wasn't going to stop until he'd squashed Oliver like a bug. *This isn't slowing him down enough to get a halter on him, that's for sure...*

In desperation, he tried the tie the shoelace spell.

The long feathery hairs on the ram's legs immediately tied themselves to each other. The ram teetered and tried to extrude another set of cloudy legs to steady himself.

*Oh no you don't!* Oliver tied that pair together too, and then the next pair.

It appeared the ram had a limit on how many legs it could manage. At eight it had an unpleasant, spidery look, but it didn't grow any more. It tried to pull one set back into its body and Oliver ignored the throbbing in his skull and tied that pair to the next pair and then to the next pair and then the ram fell over and kicked furiously.

"Now!" cried the Rain Wife.

"You got him!" Trebastion said, cheering.

Oliver staggered to his feet, halter in hand, and ran at the ram. It bucked and squirmed and he didn't dare let up on the shoelace spell. Bits of wool began to braid themselves together. The ram let out a noise that started as a bleat and ended in thunder.

He grabbed one of the ram's horns and cried out. Electricity crackled and burned in his hand and he dropped it instantly. Thunder snarled over his head.

The ram thrashed his head. *I've got to get the halter on. I can't keep this spell up much longer.*

One leg worked loose of the spell and the ram pulled it in and thrust it out again, kicking at Oliver.

*Think! Think! You did worse than this to Bill because you were frightened. Are you not scared enough now?*

He thought of Vezzo and Matty and his mother. He thought of the green plants turning dry and yellow under the punishing, rainless sky. *Oh god, what if I fail?*

He was not afraid for his life, but he could be afraid for them.

Desperation lent the spell strength. He tried to channel it, tried to narrow the spell down instead of just casting it as wide as he could. He needed the ram's head pulled back. He matted cloud wool across its neck, trying to drag its head back with its own hair, just a little more, a little more... *the dead grass crackling underfoot, the road dry as dust, the animals panting for water in the heat, he had been gone for days, how bad was the drought now, had the well gone dry yet...*

There!

Thunder roared in his ears and Oliver jammed the halter down over the ram's head and yanked the rope tight. The ram kicked a few times, sullenly. The thunder quieted. Lightning stopped crawling across the curled horns, although they still had a prickly, electric look to them.

"Well done," said Gregor.

Oliver swayed on his feet. Was his nose bleeding?

*Gushing,* said the armadillo. Oliver sighed and tried to staunch it on his sleeve.

He slowly let the shoelace spell unwind. The ram got to his feet. He tugged briefly at the halter, looking disgusted and resigned.

"Do you have to do that every time?" asked Trebastion.

"Nah," said Gregor. "Normally, we just use the dog and a bit of sweet feed."

Oliver laughed painfully. "Now you tell me!"

"You earned your rain, youngster," said the Rain Wife. "Get up on his back and get you home."

"He'll give you no more trouble," said Gregor. "Well, not much." The Cloud Herder stepped forward and gave Oliver a hand up onto the ram's back.

If there were bones underneath the wool, Oliver couldn't feel them. It was like riding a pillow. A hostile pillow, admittedly, but a pillow, nonetheless. He squeezed his knees and the ram made a grumbling thunder noise in his throat.

Gregor reached down and picked up the armadillo, settling it in Oliver's lap. "Don't forget this!" called Trebastion, holding up Oliver's pack. He limped forward and handed it over.

Oliver swallowed hard. "Trebastion..."

"Don't worry about me," said the minstrel. "I'm better off than I was by a long shot. Maybe I'll come visit you in Loosestrife."

"After we've fattened you up some," said the Rain Wife. "A strong wind could blow you away right now." Trebastion winked at Oliver.

*He'll land on his feet*, the armadillo said. *Now let's get these beasts home.*

"How do I—" he started to ask Gregor, and then the ram leapt into the sky.

⚛

Flying was not like Oliver had expected. He had always thought that it must be very windy. He had never stopped to think that the clouds moved at the same speed as the wind, so the air around them seemed very calm.

The ram raced upward, into the sky, but the lack of wind made it seem almost languorous. The Cloud Herder village fell away below them. Oliver's last glimpse of Gregor, Trebastion, and the Rain Wife was as three pale dots and a flash of blue light.

The Rainblades spread out on either side of them, a jagged-toothed comb raking the clouds. Stone outcroppings swirled with mist, as mystical and magical-looking as anything Oliver had ever pictured, even if the Cloud Herders had turned out to be something very different. He felt a pang. There was a whole world in those mountains, unlike anything he'd ever seen. He wanted to go back and explore them, to walk along the ridgelines and taste the thinness of the air.

Harkhound was a river of green under them. The wind must be very strong at ground level, he thought, because the treetops were whipping back and forth. He almost expected to see them froth like water underneath him.

He looked over his shoulder and saw the flock behind him, cloud ewes bunched together, racing after the storm cloud ram.

"Does he know where we're going?' asked Oliver.

"I'm trying to tell him," said the armadillo. "He keeps asking what it looks like from above."

"Uh..."

"Tell me about it."

Harkhound fell behind them. The dusty fields were washed out tan. From above, Oliver could see vast gray circles, like pockmarks on the earth. *Bad ground.*

They didn't look like smoke damage. He wondered if it was something fixable, perhaps if the right crops were planted, the right cantrips said. Could he pull the badness out of the earth, the way he pulled gremlin mischief from the millworks?

"That's a job for another day," said the armadillo. "Or another season."

Oliver nodded.

"Perhaps when I'm a little older," he said.

The armadillo snorted.

A thin band of green appeared on the horizon. The orchard? Still mostly green, even if the green was drying brown and the leaves were starting to curl.

Then he saw it—a thread of chimney smoke.

"There," he said, slapping the ram's cloudy shoulder. "There! Where the smoke is! That's home!"

The ram lowered its head and charged downward.

The wind caught up with them. Oliver's hair was blown back and he had to clutch at the armadillo to keep his familiar from being swept out of his arms. The ram swept so low that it seemed like he might crash into the upper branches of the orchard. Oliver sawed on the rope halter, but that only seemed to pull the ram's head sideways, not up. Oliver closed his eyes and waited for impact.

It didn't come. He pried his eyes open and looked over his shoulder. Leaves and dust whirled up from where the ram's hooves struck the upper branches and were swept away in the rising wind.

And then they were over Loosestrife. Oliver saw Vezzo's

farm and the mill and the inn and beyond that, the little rows of houses. "Here!" he said again. "Here, right here!"

The ram landed in the central square, as lightly as a blown leaf. Oliver slid off his back. The ride had taken less than ten minutes and his legs felt like jelly.

"Please," he said. "Please, this is where we need the rain."

The ram snorted and tossed his head. Thunder boomed around them like a giant pounding on a drum.

And then there was a much softer sound, a sound so quiet and yet so welcome that it rang in Oliver's ears as if it were far louder. The sound of a raindrop on the dust.

The smell of rain filled the air. Another drop landed, and another. Oliver looked up, and saw the cloud sheep prancing overhead, shedding wool that vanished into raindrops.

"Oliver?" said a voice behind him. "Oliver, did you just... fly in? On a sheep?"

He turned and saw Vezzo. The farmer stared at him, then past him at the cloud ram.

"Hi, Vezzo," he said. "I brought the rain."

Vezzo opened his mouth and then closed it again as rain began to patter down on his shoulders. A drop slid down his face like a tear. "You did," he said. "You did." He took three steps forward and threw his arms around Oliver. "You did it."

The rain began to fall harder and harder. Oliver was glad of it, because that meant that Vezzo couldn't tell that he was crying. "Yeah," he said. "Yeah, I did."

Somewhere in there, he'd dropped the rope on the ram's halter. He looked back and met the creature's flickering blue eyes.

"Thank you," he said. The ram snorted disdainfully at him and leapt into the sky. The rain's ferocity increased, and wind whipped around them. "I think there's going to be a storm," he told Vezzo.

"What?! I can't hear you!"

"A storm!" he yelled, just as lightning split the sky overhead.

The rain was coming down hard, a good solid soaking rain, the kind that filled aquifers and cisterns and irrigation ditches.

Vezzo slapped him between the shoulder blades. "Your mom's home!" he shouted and gestured down the road toward Oliver's cottage. He said something else, but all Oliver caught was "after you" and that was enough.

Oliver swept up the armadillo in his arms and began to run.

He was drenched to the skin by the time he reached the front door. The few flowers that had survived the drought were bent double under the onslaught. Water gurgled through the downspout into the rain barrels and washed the cobbles clean.

Oliver threw the door open.

His mother was sitting at the kitchen table with a whetstone, sharpening her sword. Her face was set in grim lines, the face of a woman about to go on a rescue mission, even if it cost her her life. Armor was stacked neatly across the table, ready to be donned at a moment's notice.

When the door opened, she looked up.

"Hi, Mom," he said, his arms full of armadillo. "I made it. I'm home."

# ACKNOWLEDGMENTS

I started *Minor Mage* aka "The Thing With The Armadillo" in late 2006, a time of great personal misery and, perhaps not unusually, great personal productivity. I started a good half-dozen books that I would finish over the course of years. *Minor Mage* is, I think, the last of the bunch, although I won't swear to it.

I added more to it occasionally as the years went on, and sometimes I forgot that I'd done so, so that I would open up the file and discover thousands of words that I recognized but didn't remember writing. This happens rather a lot, at least to me, and I don't think it's a sign of any particular mental dysfunction, but if it is, at least Other Me is getting the wordcount in.

I believed then and believe now that *Minor Mage* is a children's book. Various editors have attempted to disabuse me of this notion, but they were all adults and thus their opinion is suspect. (Of course, so is mine.) Eventually I realized that what many of them objected to was the idea of a twelve-year-old out on his own, driven from home by an angry mob, missing his mother and in dire peril. This is the sort of thing adults, particularly new parents, stress over. Kids are perfectly happy with it, of course, but kids, by and large, are not editors. The final call on where this book gets classified may have to lie in the hands of the reader. I'm just here to write about sarcastic armadillos.

There is a whole genre of folk ballads where a harper makes a harp or a fiddle from a murdered woman's bones, and the harp then plays aloud to accuse the murderer. Being the sort of person that I am, I started thinking about how that would work. It's not the sort of thing most people would just set out to do. You can't string a harp with someone's long golden hair, no matter what the ballads say, and a breastbone is really not the right shape for most musical instruments. Obviously magic had to be involved, and that got me thinking about how unpleasant it would be to be the victim of such magic. Bad enough that you've discovered a body, but now you're having to root around in it and make an impossible harp... (Did I mention that I still believe this is a children's book?)

The ghuls, meanwhile, sprang from a marvelous description of ghuls in *The Encyclopedia of Legendary Creatures,* a children's book illustrated by the fantastic Victor Ambrus, which gave me many glorious nightmares as a child. My mother kept threatening to take it away because it frightened me so much, but I loved it with a desperate passion. Decades later, she found a secondhand copy and mailed it to me, a gift I treasure enormously. The text is not so alarming as I recalled, but the illustrations are still superb.

So I have finally wrapped up Oliver's story, and you have either finished reading it or have flipped to the end to make sure everyone lives, in which case you've overshot a bit, but I promise everyone will be fine. Except the ghuls and Stern and you probably weren't worried about them anyway.

Getting this book out took thirteen years, as you've read, but also the input of a lot of extra people. Thanks go to my beloved editor KB Spangler, who told me repeatedly and with capital letters that this was absolutely not a children's book, but who edited it anyway; my friend Andrea the Shepherd, who cheered and clapped and also spot-checked the bits with sheep to make sure I was not doing anything too far afield from conventional shepherding (other than the cloud thing); my agent, Helen, who kept faith with the book for years despite her occasional bafflement with it; my faithful copyeditors, Sigrid, Jes A, and Cassie; and my buddies at Argyll Publications who made the lovely print version.

I hope you enjoyed it, and I hope your town always has plenty of rain.

T Kingfisher

2019

# ABOUT THE AUTHOR

T. Kingfisher is a pen-name for the Hugo-Award winning author and illustrator Ursula Vernon.

Ms. Kingfisher lives in North Carolina with her husband, garden, and disobedient pets. Using Scrivener only for e-books, she chisels the bulk of her drafts into the walls of North Carolina's ancient & plentiful ziggurats. She is fond of wombats and sushi, but not in the same way.

You can find links to all these books, new releases, artwork, rambling blog posts, links to podcasts and more information about the author at www.tkingfisher.com